"Well," **Georgie** **continues**, "then it makes perfect sense. She's disrupted your game mojo, Henry."

"Why? It's not like I got attached to her."

"Maybe not, but you liked her and she dumped you. That's never happened."

"I feel fine. I promise, no broken hearts here." Though maybe I do miss hearing Elle's snorty laugh.

"If you say so, but she's planted a seed of doubt in that thick skull of yours. So you're going to have to find a way to fix it."

But how? Elle hates me. And we fight every time we see each other. "Easier said than done."

"Not really. Whatever you did to piss her off, just apologize."

"I didn't do anything. She says we're just not right for each other and accuses me—*me* of all people—of not being a man."

My sister frowns and rubs her pointed little chin. "Hmmm…then man up. Show her you're not afraid to grovel a little. If that doesn't work, then hit her with the old Henry charm. I've yet to see a girl resist you when you act like an actual human being."

OTHER WORKS BY MIMI JEAN PAMFILOFF

OH, HENRY

THE OHELLNO SERIES
BOOK TWO

MIMI JEAN PAMFILOFF

A Mimi Boutique Novel

Cover Design by Earthly Charms (www.earthlycharms.com)
Creative Editing by Latoya C. Smith (lcsliterary.com)
Line Editing and Proof Reading by Pauline Nolet (www.paulinenolet.com)
Formatting by bbebooksthailand.com

OH, HENRY

PROLOGUE

HENRY

Austin, Texas. Alpha Phi Frat House.

"Sorry, Henry, but I don't owe you an explanation. It's over, and that's all there is to it." Elle's big brown eyes show zero emotion, so I put on my game face. I've never been chucked like this. Never. Because I'm fucking Henry Walton, one of four heirs to the Walton oil fortune, famously handsome, and the most anticipated NFL college draft pick since that asshole who got signed with the Steelers.

Elle's giant brain must be broken.

Standing in the doorway of our two-story, Southern-charmer of a frat house, I step outside in my Pirates PJs bottoms onto the porch. I carefully close the door so the guys inside, who are fellow Pirates, don't overhear. They'd never let this go. Football players live to fuck with each other.

"You—*you're* rejecting *me?*" I point to my bare chest, snarling down at her little round face. Sure, she's got a genius IQ and is the likeliest person to build a tele-transporter or some geeky *Star Trek* shit like that, but I'm what the ladies call a bona fide catch. Six-five, two hundred and eighty pounds of pure muscle pleasure, orgasm philanthropist, future football Hall of Famer, and—fucking bonus point—I'm an all-around fun guy. Elle can't deny it. My ability to turn her frowns into smiles is irrefutable. It's the reason she bought that raffle ticket, the prize being a date with me, during our fraternity fundraiser. It's the reason she said she wanted me to show her a good time after she won. Which I did. Several "good times" in one night and about fifty more "*Oh, Henrys!*" since then.

So why is she dumping me? Not that we were official. *But, dammit all to hell, I like her. I really fucking like her.* Normally, I don't go nerd, but Elle suckered me with her cute little gap-toothed smile and spunky personality. Okay, and she's a blonde, which I like, and she has nice jugs.

I swallow down a tangled mess in my throat. "Fine. Plenty of fish in the sea. I'm cool with that."

"Errr...you don't look cool. Do you need to sit?"

"Just a hangover," I lie. "Big party last night." Actually, I can't remember what I did. I can't think straight.

Elle touches my arm, pity written all over her face. "Henry, we were never really going to work out. Even you had to know that."

I slowly remove her hand. "Never gave it much

thought." *Too busy living the dream and all that.*

She shoves her petite hands into her pink overalls. "Well, I need more than a hot guy with big muscles. I need..." She blows out a long breath. "I need a man. One who will be there when things get difficult. One who's had to deal with the real world. You only know screwing and football, and I respect that. I might even be jealous. But there is no universe in which your interests and mine could coalesce into a symbiotic relationship outside the bedroom."

"Who says you even *symbiotified* me there?" No. That's not a real word. And we both know I could fuck Elle all day long and never get tired of her. There's this little squeaking thing that she does right before she's about to come. Adorable.

Wait. No. Fuck that. It's annoying. Just like her shrill laugh, obsession with spy novels, and stupid nerd jokes about black holes—*"Two protons walk into a black hole, blah, blah, stupid science punch line, blah, blah."*

Good riddance.

But as I think those words, something deep inside sets off like a grenade. Boom. I'm pissed. I just can't fuckin' believe that she's kicking my awesome ass to the curb and won't even tell me why. Not the real truth anyway. Because even a guy like me with *only* above average intelligence can see that Elle's little line about needing "a man" is bullshit. Men just don't come any manlier than me.

Elle laughs, followed by a little squeak. My eyes zero in on that gap between her teeth. How had I thought that was hot? She looks nothing like a young Madonna.

Yeah, she looks more like Urkel. Only pale as shit with blonde pigtails and tape in the middle of her glasses. I'm the one who actually broke them, though. I sat on them after we screwed. She kind of got mad, and I offered to replace them ten times, but she just shrugged it off. "No biggie. What's a nerd without a little tape? I'll fix 'em later," she said.

Elle finishes honking out a final laugh. I can't believe I'm into her.

Was into her.

"Symbiotified. Oh, Henry. I'm going to miss your humor." She grabs my arm and gives it a squeeze. "It was nice knowing you."

I jerk my head. "Been nice knowing you, too. Good luck with your…math 'n shit."

Fuck. That sounded lame.

Elle crinkles her nose. "Yeah. I'll cross my fingers and hope those big scary numbers finally make sense." She turns away and heads toward campus, shaking her tight little ass in her overalls.

Jesus, what was I even doing with her? I can get tens—ten cheerleaders, ten models, or ten of the hottest women at any party.

I snarl at the back of her head and clench my fists. "Stupid geek!"

Without slowing her pace or turning around,

she throws up a middle finger. "Dumb jock!"

I can't help but laugh. She may look like a helpless, lost little nerd begging for social ridicule, but I've yet to meet anyone with bigger balls. Male or female.

Stop it, Henry. It's over. I gush out a breath of frustration. *Fuck her. I don't need anything but football.*

CHAPTER ONE

Four weeks later.

"Walton! Get your sorry ass over here!" the coach yells, cutting our play short and eliciting a mixture of groans and "eat me, Waltons!" from my fellow Pirates.

I don't know why I'm in my worst slump ever. I really don't. Play says go right, I go left. When I'm supposed to block left, I put my head up my ass. It's like my brain is scrambled or something.

"Fulking herl," I mumble, spitting out my mouthpiece and releasing my chin strap. This is the seventh play I've fucked up this practice, and it wanes in comparison to the chunky-style cluster I created during our last game versus San Diego. And the game before that with LA. And the game before that with Notre Dame—we lost that one. The other games were close calls. Too close.

"Hey, man, it's okay. Everyone has a bad streak," says Hunter. He's the new starting quarter-back, so not as big of a dude as me, but a damned good player especially for a freshman. The topper? He's a damned good friend too—something I never expected to gain out of this shit storm more unaffectionately referred to as the sinking SS *Henry*.

But I'm not a quitter.

Never have been.

Never will be.

I'll do anything to turn my ship around, even leaving the coveted Alpha Phi frat house a few weeks ago. With my head in such a bad place, I decided I might be due for a change. That and the parties every night were getting on my last iron-pumping, protein-shake-fueled nerve.

"Walton! You deaf or something?" the coach yells, still standing on the sidelines, waiting to chew me out.

I look over at Hunter, whose face is all soured up, like he's cringing on my behalf. He knows, just like I do, that the coach doesn't want me here anymore because I've been playing like a moron. Of course, he needs me too much, and luckily, my agent says no one else is worried. The offer to sign with the Texans after graduation is still on the table.

"Uh-oh, Pretty Boy Liam's in trouble," one of the guys sings teasingly.

I fucking hate it when they call me that. I do not look like Liam Hemsworth. I am definitely Chris. But bigger.

"Shut it, asshole," I tell the guy and remove my helmet. I jog over to Coach Newton—a short bald dude with shit-brown eyes. "Hey, Coach, I know that wasn't great, but I'm working on it—"

"You're out, Walton."

My gut fills with cement. "Out? You can't make me sit out. I need to practice, not jerk off on the bench."

"No, jackass. You're out for the season. Take a seat." He points his finger in my face. "And don't start, Walton. I warned you, so you've only brought this on yourself."

I am literally speechless. This is my fourth season playing for the Pirates, and my stats have put this team on the map. The publicity alone has attracted new players with solid pro potential, like Hunter, and Coach Newton is now hailed as the best college coach in the country. Everyone is living the dream, thanks to me. Okay, and it doesn't hurt that my family donates a few million each year to the school. We have the best equipment, best facilities, best everything.

I cross my arms over my chest and snarl down at Coach Newton. I may be a college student, but I'm no child. I know the score. I know my value. "You bench me and you're the one who's going to look like a jackass. Everyone's going to put this on you— your inability to manage one of your star players. Then there's the fact that the university chairs won't be happy. The Waltons are key donors."

Coach Newton's sunburnt nostrils flare, and his right eye twitches. "That a threat, Walton?"

"No, sir, just a fact. A fact like any other. Including how I could've switched schools and taken my money with me. A fact like I've been playing flawless defense for almost four seasons and nothing will get more guys signed and bring in more money for the school than me." I point to my chest. "*Me* getting drafted for ten mil a year." It's a three-year contract, so that adds up to a nice sum, but I'm not in it for the money. I love the game and have since I was old enough to walk.

"Look, Walton," Coach hisses quietly, "no one is going to deny what you've brought to the table, but I'm not putting the championship at risk because *you* suddenly decided to act like a chimpanzee rolling around in his own shit."

Dick. My playing isn't *that* bad. I'm more like an untamed stallion. Who's forgotten how to run. "I thought chimps wore diapers," I say.

"Shut up, Walton!" He points a stubby finger in my face. "I don't know what's gotten in your head, and I don't care. I've given you a month to turn it around, but you keep playing like a little cunt, which means we'll lose the season. All of us."

Fuck. I run a hand over the top of my sweaty hair. I can't really argue with his logic. If I keep screwing up, our team won't go to the play-offs, and that'll make us all look bad.

I kick at the muddy grass. "Yeah, well. That's not what I want."

"That's a good boy." Newton goes to his tiptoes

and taps the top of my head. "Knew you'd see it my way. Now take a seat." Coach turns and walks away.

Good boy? And did he just pat me on the head like a dog?

"But I'm still playing!" I belt out.

The coach stops in his tracks and slowly turns to face me.

"Hey, don't look at me." I throw him a snide grin. "You're the one who says 'quitter' is just another word for giant pussy." I smile and point to my crotch. "And I'm not seein' pussy down there, Coach."

Just one big dick. Which I've had to be in order to get where I am. Because despite growing up in a privileged family, I've had to fight tooth and nail every step of the way.

I put on my helmet and walk past him, giving him a slap on the ass. "Thanks for the pep talk, Dana. Just what I needed."

Dana is his first name. We think Coach hates it because it's a chick's name, too.

My teammates eye me in silence as I take my place on the field, head down, fingers pushed into the mud.

"You okay?" Hunter asks, coming up to my side.

"Never better. Let's play."

Hunter stands there for a moment too long, like he wants to say something, but then leaves.

Good choice.

The guys line up, some playing offense and facing us.

I can do this. I can make this play. I have to believe that. I have to push out the noise in my head that keeps me from being here and nowhere else.

Focus, Henry. Focus. I can't keep letting everyone down. Not when their dreams are on the line, too. Most of us have worked since we were ten to get here—the last stop on the way to pro. And there is no sweeter glory than doing what you love for a living, even if it's just for a few short years. It's what we've all been killing ourselves for: The chance to say "I did it. I made it."

I feel the soft grass and cool mud beneath my fingertips, and the air fills with a ferocious calm as everyone prepares for the play. I feel the energy spike all around me while my thoughts melt away. Here on the field, there are no tests to cram for, no wars, no angry girlfriends or psycho parents. The only thing that matters is this field where we become one. *One team. One goal. One team. One goal…*

Suddenly, I'm there. In the zone. And the rush feels like nirvana—a moment of peace and silence so fragile yet so vivid and alive that my entire body electrifies, like I'm touching God or plugged into some supernatural energy.

Playing opposite us, I hear Hunter call the hike, and the moment of serenity shatters like a plate-glass window that's met with a brick. Grunts and snarls fill the air as I charge at my teammate, Jon, who's playing tight end and trying to create an opening for the running back so Hunter can pass. There is no doubt in my mind I can block Jon. I'm faster and stronger. No one gets around me. Not ever. That's what I tell myself, anyway.

I plow into Jon, who goes flying back, landing with a thud on his ass. I keep going, rushing toward an opening right through the guards. Hunter is about to make his throw, and I barrel into his chest, knocking him clean into next Sunday.

"Fucker!" Hunter barks from underneath me.

I chuckle and roll off him.

"Jesus, Henry. You nearly took my head off," he says.

"It's a beautiful thing." I hop to my feet and offer Hunter a hand.

His blue eyes are crisp with anger as I yank him up, but the moment he's on his feet, his expression turns into a glib smirk.

"Looks like someone's here to see you," he says, looking over my shoulder.

I turn, and there she is, sitting on the bleachers. I could spot her thick-framed hipster glasses and honey blonde hair from a mile away.

Elle. Oh, man. Why's she here?

"Christ," Hunter chuckles his words. "What is she wearing?"

Her T-shirt has a huge picture of a grey-and-white cat with its head tilted to one side.

"Yeah, that's Mr. Nucleus." I clear my throat. "He was hit by a car last year."

"She's wearing a picture of her dead cat?"

I nod. It's one of Elle's many eccentricities. She seems unable to accept that Mr. Nucleus is gone, like she's not good at dealing with death or something. I once tried asking her about it, but she'd simply replied by telling me that death is just one more mystery of the universe she hopes to solve. "You can't solve death, Elle. It's not a math problem," I had told her, but she'd just shrugged and changed subjects.

Anyway, I think it's kind of sweet, the way she loves her cat and doesn't want to forget him. Still, "If you think the cat shirt is interesting, you should see her unicorn T-shirt collection. It's magical," I say dryly because it's not. It's fucking horrible. All glittery 'n shit.

The coach blows the whistle to return us to formation, and I hustle. That had been a perfect play, and I don't want to waste time getting back into my groove. My mind has suddenly snapped into place and everything feels right. I don't even mind that Elle is here.

"Let's play, boys," I say, and get into position.

ELLE

It's Friday, the last day of classes before Thanksgiving break, and I'm not exactly sure why I've come to see Henry practice, considering that I told him we were through. Maybe part of me longs for a little stress relief, the reason I began seeing him initially. I had never had casual sex before him, but nothing in my life has plotted normal this past year, and now I'm nervous about going home for an entire week. The two-hour drive isn't far, so I go home all the time to see my poor mother, who has a brain tumor and is in the process of evolving away from this world. At least, that's the way I like to think of it. When it's our time, we transform, but we never truly die.

Matter can't die.

Of course, if my heart believed all that, I wouldn't have to remind myself fifteen times a day that death is part of life or that my mother can't leave this world seeing me a mess. Her final happiness is why I started college at the age of nineteen after swearing I'd never go. She's why I've stuck with it and pretend things are normal. Pretending is also how I handle seeing her for a day or two before running back to campus, where I erect my mental fortress and make it all go away.

Thanksgiving week, though… Ugh. My aunt and uncle from California will be there, as will my cousin. My older sister, Lana, who lives nearby, and my father will be there, too, of course. But I know this upcoming week, likely our last Thanksgiving with her, is going to feel more like a funeral, not a holiday. Because my family's not like me. They're not able to bury their emotions in a sea of logic. I'll have to sit there and listen to the sadness in their voices and see the tears. Then I'll have to watch my mother trying to stay strong for them when I know on the inside, nothing hurts her more than watching the people she loves suffer.

How am I going to get through this?

Crap. It's no wonder I find myself longing for Henry. Mr. Fun. He's also the hottest guy I've ever met. Tall and strong like a great oak, vivid green eyes, dirty blond hair, and a panty dropper of a smile. My roomie, Tassie, says he looks like a seriously built, young Brad Pitt. I just say the man is fine. *Sigh...*

I watch Henry's towering hulk of a frame mow down two guys on the field; one of them is Hunter. Hunter is tall and lean with dark hair and blue eyes. He's cute, hotheaded, and has a serious heart-on for Tassie, who is currently not speaking to him. It's a mess, really. Anyone can see that Hunter and Tass are madly in love and have been since they were little. They grew up next door to each other and somehow ended up at the same college.

Anyway, Tass has become a good friend, which is why I feel bad for having lied to her. She has no clue I kept seeing Henry after she had her fallout with Hunter and their frat did the unthinkable. But there hasn't been a good time to tell her until recently—she's been too upset.

Well, maybe it's time to clear the air. And since I'm here, I can warn Henry. Yes, a great excuse for being here since I can't tell Henry the real reason. I kinda miss him.

I lean back and watch the cheerleading squad— all Gamma Nu sorority sisters—doing flips on the side of the field. I suddenly wonder which one of these incredibly beautiful women with perfect thighs, boobs, and legs is keeping Henry's bed warm at night. He's an animal in the sack, completely insatiable, and words cannot describe how much I miss the stress relief he brought to my life. No, he has no clue about my mom, and I have no intention of ever telling him. I need him and everything related to school to remain isolated from that part of my life.

Practice wraps up with the blow of the coach's whistle, and the sweaty, tired-looking team makes their way to the locker room. Everyone except Henry, who's high-fiving a few ladies as he heads toward me and the bleachers.

My heart rate increases, and little flutters erupt inside my knotted stomach. I don't know what I want to say to him. Somehow, I doubt I'll muster the courage to spit out, "I needed to see your smiling face." Besides, it wouldn't be fair. He'll think it means something more than it does when I already know he's not the guy for me.

I get up and take the stairs to meet up with Henry on the side of the grassy field.

"Hey," I say with false bravado.

He pops off his helmet and those stunning green eyes of his sparkle in the sunlight. He's so full of life. I love that about him.

"Hey, Elle." His voice is deep, like a growling bear, and exactly what you'd expect from a guy who's six-five and over twice my size.

A flash of memories explodes inside my mind of Henry groaning in my ear, telling me how beautiful I am, and of him laughing with that gruff-sounding voice as he pins me down and tickles my neck with his stubbly chin. Henry loved making me laugh.

Suddenly, I realize that moments have passed and we're just standing there staring at each other's lips.

I shake it off and clear my throat. "I, uh, just came by to say hi. How's it going?"

He flashes one of those dimply, scruffy-jaw smiles that make my panties instantly steam up. "Surprisingly well, actually." He makes a little shrug with his wide shoulders, the padding underneath his black jersey making him look even bigger than he already is.

"I'm happy to hear that," I lie, secretly wanting him to be miserable without me.

Stupid. You don't want that. Get your head out of your rear orifice, Elle.

He nods and stares like he's waiting.

"Oh. Yeah, I, uh…just wanted you to know that I'm going to come clean with Tass."

"About what?" he asks.

"About you and me. I mean, I know it's over, but I never told her the truth, and I think I should now that she seems to be turning the corner."

"What corner?" he asks.

"Hunter. She's finally starting to get over him—I think—and I really don't like keeping secrets from her."

The atmosphere abruptly shifts between us, and his eyes harden on me, like he expected me to give him another reason for my visit.

Oh, crap. I've made a huge selfish mistake by coming here. Whatever happened between us, we're still not over it. Yet nothing's changed. I'm wrong for him. He's wrong for me.

"Fine by me," he says. His tone is sharp and accusatory. "I never told you to lie to her—that was all you. I just went along to make you happy. Clearly, that's not possible."

The jab isn't missed, but I need to steer clear of the "us" topic and get the hell out of here. Fast.

"And I thank you for helping me protect her. She would've felt betrayed if she'd known I kept seeing you after Hunter slept with her for a bet."

It's true, and the infamous bet is also a good reminder of why Henry is so, so, soooo wrong for me. As part of rush week, there'd been a stupid frat game involving stealing things from other Greeks, hazing, drinking, and nailing virgins. The pledges with the highest scores became the newest members of the Alpha Phi fraternity, which is the big football frat that Henry, and now Hunter, belong to. *Lame.*

Henry shakes his head and drags his strong hand over the top of his sweaty blond mop. He's the only man in the world whose perspiration comes out smelling like spring water infused with mint or something herbal. He always smells good.

"You're wrong," he says. "Hunter didn't fuck Tass for a bet. He's into her. Period. And we both know that."

"Yeah, well, he might be into her, but he still participated in the bet, and you can't argue that it looks bad." Henry has three sisters—two older and one younger—so I know he gets what I'm saying.

"It did look bad," he admits, "which is why a bunch of us left the frat, despite knowing we'd piss off half the team."

"Really?"

"Yes. Really."

"Why?" I ask, hardly able to believe it.

"I can't speak for the other guys, but I'm twenty-two and a senior. Doing the same old shit from freshman year just didn't make sense anymore."

Wow. My stomach does this little cramping thing that causes a chain reaction, ending in my rapidly beating heart. Henry's leaving the Alphas takes our romantic equation one step closer to a positive integer. Sadly, however, the facts that football is his life, he doesn't possess a sympathetic bone in his body, and he's more narcissistic than an only child who's a runway model keep our equation in the negative five thousands with regards to chances of succeeding as a couple. Still, Henry's leaving the Alphas is huge.

"When did this happen?" I ask.

"A few weeks ago. Hunter, me, and two other guys got an apartment."

"Hunter, too?" I can't wait to tell Tassie since I'm sure she was the catalyst and she's never truly going to be happy until she and Hunter make up.

"Hey, who can resist living with me? Plus, my family owns the building, so rent is cheap."

"Plus you get more privacy for your orgies."

"Exactly," he says. "We're having one tonight. Just us dudes and fifty women. Want to be number fifty-one?"

I make a gag sound.

"Elle, that was a joke. We haven't even had one party."

"Yeah, right." I let out *pffft!* That's like saying he's joined a circus but doesn't plan to put on a red nose or make balloon animals. Or ride in a tiny car. Or make children laugh. *Or scream, depending on their feelings about clowns.*

Don't go there, Elle. Let go of your colorful past.

Henry crosses his big, big arms over his big, big chest. "I'm serious. We're a no-party, study-only bachelor pad. Why's that so hard to believe?"

"Because you live for that bullcrap."

His nostrils flare a little, and his normally

plump lips go flat.

"Fine. Whatever." I hold up two palms in surrender. "I didn't come here to talk about that, and if it's true, then I'm happy for you. I think it'll be good for you academically speaking, because God knows you could use some improvement."

"Elle," his light brown brows pull together, "there's nothing wrong with my academics."

I laugh. "You have a three point three GPA, Henry."

Wait. That came out sounding really bitchy, didn't it?

"Wow." He shakes his head. "That was bitchy."

Okay. Mea culpa. Still, how dare he call me that!

I feel my claws extend. "I can't help it if I find your lack of ambition to be comical," I say calmly. "Besides, I'm sure you're used to bitches—since you date the cream of the crop." I glance over at the cheerleaders, three of whom are watching us and snickering. I know they think I'm just fan-girling over him or trying to trade math tutoring for sex. They wouldn't ever believe that a guy like him would voluntarily be with a super-nerd like me.

Actually, come to think of it, maybe I don't believe it either. Just like I don't believe he could ever make me happy. *There. You see, Elle. You made the right choice dumping him.*

"That wasn't nice. Since when did you get so bitter?"

"Must be the company," I reply.

He shakes his head and throws in a *tsk-tsk* for good measure. "I don't know what I ever saw in you."

His words instantly sting, which shocks me because I'm not new to insults. For example, my nickname in high school was "shark bait." Yes, from the movie *Nemo*. I skipped a bunch of grades, which made me very small compared to my much older peer group. For demonstration purposes, I'll disclose that I literally wore a training bra at my high school graduation. And it was too big. I really needed an over-the-shoulder pebble holder.

Well, that was then and this is now. I'm almost twenty and all filled out. *And I don't need Henry's approval.*

I lift my chin and meet Henry's angry green eyes. "Well, I know exactly what I saw in you." I reach for the bulge between his powerful thighs. He's wearing an athletic supporter, so his footballs look even bigger than they are. But make no mistake, his sporting goods section is as big as a girl like me—who's five two and weighs one hundred and twenty pounds—can tackle.

I give his man gear a little squeeze, and his whole body freezes up, like he's sure I'm going to rip off his manhood.

"The truth is, Henry, I stopped seeing you because your goal post isn't stiff enough to keep me entertained."

Unexpectedly, Henry cups my left breast. "I know exactly how you feel. There's just not enough there to hold my interest. Guess I'll have to find a girl with adult-sized pom-poms to inspire me." The right side of his mouth curls into a cocky smile.

"Ugh!" I pull my hand from his package and slap his paw from my boob. "You're a pig."

"Yep."

"Well, I hope your *little*—" I glance at his bulge "—sense of humor keeps you warm at night when your brain is dead from all those concussions in two years."

"Don't you worry, sweetheart," he says, letting his Texan twang break loose and looking over his shoulder at a group of pom-pom-toting girls drooling over him, "stayin' warm ain't my problem." He turns and struts his rock-hard ass toward the locker room, like he owns the fucking world.

My innards sizzle with anger. "Dumb jock."

He lifts his middle finger without bothering to face me. "See ya, gorgeous."

He didn't call me a stupid nerd, but his tone said it all.

As I watch him disappear into the locker room, I can't help feeling like the tiny part of me he'd brought back to life—the part that loved to laugh and play—has just died a sad, twitchy little death. If there's anyone in the world I wanted to connect with more, it was him. But this reaffirms my earlier assumption. We don't work and never will. I need a serious guy who's my equal.

Henry is a man-child. *So hmph! Good riddance. Again.*

CHAPTER TWO

HENRY

"Evil, four-eyed troll…" I growl under my breath, grabbing my duffel bag from my locker.

The other guys on the team are busy showering off or busting each other's balls, so no one notices my fuck of a mood except for Hunter, who's just come from the coach's office.

"Hey, you okay?" Hunter asks.

"Fine." I pull my clean clothes from my bag and start removing my jersey.

"You don't look fine. What did Elle say?"

"Nothing," I snap.

"Okay, man, if you say so. But Coach wants to see you."

"Great. Just what I need," I grumble. I don't know if I'm more pissed off by what Elle just said to me or that she showed up out of the blue and ruined what would've been a perfect day. I mean, I've been waiting to get my head back in the game for weeks. She's probably jinxed me again. Not that I'm superstitious, but we all know that psychology plays an important role in winning, and my performance out there today was a direct result of…well, I don't really know. Everything just clicked again. *Fucking Elle. Why'd she have to show up?* Not like I've missed her. Much.

"You played really good out there, Henry. I'm sure that's all the coach wants to tell you," Hunter says.

"Doubtful. But tell him I'll be right there."

"Sure." Hunter disappears, and I remove my shoulder pads, trying to calm myself. It won't do me any good if I go in there ready to pick a fight that should've been left outside with that irritating chick.

I reach into my bag for my clean clothes, and out falls my lucky ring. I found it on the field right before my first game here at Austin U. I had put it in my pocket, and we won. Ever since then, I wear it taped to my chest during games for good luck. Well, I used to until I started making us lose last month. After a few weeks, I just put it away. Maybe the magic wore off. Not that I'm superstitious or anything.

Shirtless, I go into Coach's office, which has room enough for his desk and a small couch. On the wall behind him are pictures of the team, of him holding a championship trophy from last year—a trophy I helped bring home—and of his wife and daughter during some costume party. They remind me of the little people from *The Wizard of Oz*, short and dressed like they're from another world.

"Hey, Coach, what's up?" I ask.

Shuffling some papers, he looks up from his cluttered desk. "Close the door and take a seat, Walton."

I quickly eye the old plaid couch with mystery stains—some brown, some white, none of them good.

"I'm all sweaty. I'll stand." I shut the door behind me.

"Fine. Suit yourself, Walton. But I wanted to have a frank discussion about what happened on the field out there today."

"What happened was I played like a rock star." *True. Yay, me.*

He holds up one sausage-like finger. "One practice. You played one lousy practice. I wanna see you play like that during a game."

"I will."

"That's what you say, but I can't risk it. We've got less than a month left in the season. If we lose one more time, we'll be shut out from the play-offs. I'd be irresponsible to let that happen."

"Then let me play, and if you see one mistake, pull me. Hell, I'll bench myself."

Coach shakes his head and runs a tiny hand over his chrome dome. "I don't know, Walton."

"Look. We are not going to lose a game because I make one small mistake."

"You don't know that. Some games come down to one bad play."

"Or a good one. I won't let you down." I hope but don't really know. Still, "You owe me just one more shot."

His brown eyes narrow and twitch in contemplation. "Fine. But one wrong move, you're out."

"Deal."

"And you won't give me a hard time?" he adds.

"No." I shake my head. "I'll even take the heat off you with the board. I'll make sure they know I support your decision to pull me. If it comes to that," I add. "But it won't." I fucking hope.

Coach Newton nods. "Okay, Walton. Take this week and get some rest. We have a big game after the break and I want to see your best playing."

I nod. "Thanks, Coach."

He grumbles something under his breath, and I reach for the door handle.

"Hey, Walton, what made you change out there today? It's not like that was the first time I've yelled at you."

I stop and think about it. "I'm not really sure. I guess I really just wanted to play."

"Are you saying you didn't want that before?" he asks.

"No. Of course not."

"Then I suggest you take a good hard look at what got your head back in the game. Had to be something."

He's right. It did have to be something. But what? I didn't change anything. I played liked shit, felt like shit, the coach yelled at me, I yelled back, and then I played like perfection. Like everything was right in the world and nothing could stop—

Fuck. It hits me like a gas station sushi. *I saw Elle.* She was the only new thing.

"Feeling sick, Walton?" the coach barks.

"Uh, no. I'm fine."

"Then why do you look green?"

I blink. *Because I think I know why everything went south on me.* It all started after nerd queen dumped me. And then, just like that, she shows up and I'm fine.

No. No. No. Ohellno. She can't be my lucky charm. I refuse to let it be her.

Sadly, however, all facts point in one direction. And dammit, she's way too big to strap to my chest during a game.

No, man. Don't go there. There has to be some other reason I played so well. Besides, Elle was nothing but a fling. A few fun fucks.

But if that's true, then why am I feeling like this? Like she somehow got under my skin and I never realized it until now.

Five weeks earlier.

Lying naked in my bed, the noise of my frat brothers all around us—loud music, laughter, and the tapping of a Ping-Pong paddle against a little plastic ball downstairs—Elle lets out a satisfied sigh. We just fucked. Hard. And the look on her oval little face with those glossy brown eyes tells me she really liked it.

Of course I have to hear it, because, well, I'm a guy.

"How was it?" I ask.

She snuggles her warm body against mine, pressing her breasts against my ribs and laying her cheek over my pec. "It was satisfactory, I guess."

What? I look down at her smirking pink lips, all swollen from kissing. "Satisfactory, huh?"

"Yeah, adequate. That's what I'd call it. Or maybe tolerable is a better word."

She's messing with me. I had her squealing for three whole minutes. I'm pretty sure the guys downstairs thought there was a mouse in my room.

Or a drowning cat.

"Yeah, I suppose you're right," I say. "Tolerable fits."

With a little laugh, she glances up at me, leaving her head resting on my chest. I like the way we feel together. It's like her little parts were made to fit perfectly with all my big parts, except down there. It takes a while to work the old sledgehammer inside so he can pound out those Os.

"Henry?" she asks with a sweet voice.

"No. I'm not ready to go again."

"I wasn't going to ask that, but darn. I'm in the mood for another round."

"Give me thirty minutes." That's code for another hour. Maybe two. She's tapped me out, and after the game today, I need my rest. "But what did you want to ask?"

"Remember when we first met at your fundraiser thing?"

How could I forget? I had just done the charity keg run, which is where we all race around a track, carrying kegs of beer. Everyone bets on which guy from our frat will win. The person who picks the winning horse gets their name put into a drawing for a date. With the winner. And, of course, I won. So when they drew the lucky ticket, I had expected some hot cheerleader from the Gamma Nus to come up and claim her prize: me. To my surprise, though, this little blonde chick with pigtails and chunky glasses, wearing a T-shirt with Elvis riding a dinosaur, marched right up to me.

"I won." She handed me the ticket.

"Errrr…"

"Here. Check the number." She shoved the ticket in my face, and I took the thing, but didn't look at it. I mean, no one else had come to claim the prize and this girl clearly meant business.

"Okay. So…let me get this straight. You want to go on a date? With me?"

She crinkled her perky little nose. "I'm cashing in my ticket, aren't I?"

"Yeah, but—"

"But what? You too good to take a nerd on a

date? You afraid of smart women?"

No. But I'm afraid of you. She was like a little pit bull. In overalls. I kind of liked it. "Just as long as you're not intimidated by my love of sports and...what's your major?"

"Physics."

Of course it is. "Just as long as you're not intimidated by my lack of interest in physics."

She laughed, but it was more like a squeak, followed by a snort.

Is this chick for real? I mean, she was a cliché from every nerd movie I'd ever seen—*Revenge of the Nerds* (Parts I, II, III, and IV), *The 40-Year-Old Virgin, Never Been Kissed* (my older sister, Michelle, made me see that one), *Napoleon Dynamite, Super Bad, Breakfast Club* (another Michelle film), *Honey, I Shrunk the Kids,* and *Weird Science.*

Her very strange laughter died down, and she placed her hand on my arm. "Silly boy. You can't intimidate me, and I have no interest in talking."

"Then what do you want to do on our date?"

She pulled a pen from her pocket protector, which was inserted into the front pouch of her overalls, and then grabbed the ticket from me. She jotted something down on the back and then returned the ticket to my hand. "I want to do you. Meet me tomorrow at two. That's my dorm room number."

She then strutted away with a confident swagger, leaving me standing there.

"Wow," I remember thinking. I loved her big balls.

"Henry?" Elle gives me a little nudge, still waiting for me to tell her if I remember the first time we met only a few weeks ago.

I shrug, trying to play it cool. "I vaguely recall you forcing yourself on me. Why?"

"No reason."

"Of course there's a reason. Otherwise you wouldn't have asked," I say.

"Don't use logic on me. It won't work."

"Why? Are you illogical?" I ask.

She smacks my bare chest, but it doesn't sting. "Har, har. You know I meant that pushing won't get me to answer."

"Well, maybe this will." I quickly grab her and roll her under me, pinning her arms over her head. "Talk, or you know what comes next."

Her big brown eyes go wide. "Oh, God. Please don't tickle me."

"I will. You know I will. Now, talk," I release one of her hands and grip her right under her rib cage, making her half-squeal, half-laugh.

"No! Henry, no!" She wiggles, trying to get away, but it's useless. I'm way bigger than she is.

"Tell me." I keep tickling her, mostly because hearing her goofy laugh makes me laugh.

"Okay! Okay. I just wanted to know if you still see me the same way."

I let her go, and she takes a deep breath.

"In what way?" I ask.

"You know, like…some leper from another planet."

Why would she say that? "Elle, I never thought that. Not once. I thought you were cute."

She crinkles her nose. "Really?"

"Yeah. Plus you basically demanded to have your way with me, so how could I resist?"

"So it was all about the sex."

I dip my head and nuzzle the little spot on her neck, right below her earlobe. "I took one look at you and thought that you were a nerd goddess I needed to bed immediately."

Elle pushes me off her and sits up. She's not smiling anymore, and I'm not sure where the conversation took a bad turn. But there's no mistaking the angry pucker on her pink lips.

"And now, Henry? What about now?" she says with a bite to her tone.

"Elle, what's this about? I thought we were having fun together."

She crosses her arms over her chest, and her eyebrows arch so high they look like they're trying to jump off her forehead. "Fun?"

Is this a trick question? "Yes, Elle. I have fun with you. I'm not seeing why you're getting upset."

"What happens when we get tired of just having fun?"

Oh no. I draw a slow breath, wondering how we got on the relationship topic so soon. We've only been seeing each other for a few weeks, and that's been nothing but sex. Okay, and we talk. She's interesting and has all sorts of crazy ideas about time travel, gene mutation, and where we really go when we die. The woman is smart with just enough crazy to make me believe her theories. Still, we've only just met.

"I don't know, Elle. What would *you* like to happen?"

She stares at the wall for a long, awkward moment. "Actually, I don't know."

Good. Then that makes two of us. "Then can't we just keep doing this and see where it goes? I mean, I'm not exactly boyfriend material. You know that."

"You mean, you're a man whore."

"No," I protest. "I'm a healthy, red-blooded, twentysomething guy. I've slept with the appropriate amount of women."

Her face gets even redder.

Oops. Wrong answer?

"And how many people have you slept with since you met me?" she asks, her tone riddled with accusation.

I really haven't wanted to see anyone but her—complete shock—but I'm just not ready to admit it. If she knew what my family was like and how they use my loyalty against me, she'd understand that trust isn't my strong suit. I mean, yeah, I have my football bros, but that's different. Everyone knows the rules. Everyone follows them: We don't ask for much and we put the game first. Easy.

"How many, Henry?"

"I don't see the point in answering, Elle. Either way, you're still going to be pissed because I'm not telling you whatever it is you want to hear and you're not willing to hear what I have to say." It's almost like she wants us to fight. She wants an excuse to walk away. *But didn't she just kind of say that she's not exactly ready for a commitment either?* I'm thoroughly lost.

Elle starts dressing, pulling on her "My President is a Unicorn" T-shirt and jeans, not bothering with the panties or bra. She shoves those items into her pockets.

"Come on, Elle. Don't leave like this." I think what we have isn't good. It's great. But I'm not willing to go all in simply because we've had a few fun weeks.

"I have to study for my chem test." She slides on her orange low tops and then sits on the edge of the bed to lace them.

"Will I see you later?"

"I'll call you." She storms from the room, not bothering to look at me.

"Bye!" I bark out, feeling my head spinning.

Instant replay:

- She backed me into a corner about our future.

- I opted for honesty and she sort of agreed with me.

- That made her mad.

Okay. I'm lost. I feel like I've traveled to a foreign country inhabited only by women, and have somehow managed to violate a rule of the natives. Only, I don't speak their language, so I can't fix it or apologize.

Dude. Whatever. I was honest with her, and if she doesn't want to be honest with me, then fine. I don't have time for games. Except football.

CHAPTER THREE
HENRY

Present Day.

My parents' annual Texan turkey trot charity dinner is always held on a Wednesday and is always a dog-and-pony show where they invite a hundred of their "closest" richest friends to our house in River Oaks, an exclusive neighborhood in Houston, for a formal dinner.

While my parents, Chester and Georgina, schmooze for donations and they all pretend not to talk about business, my three sisters—Claire, Michelle, and little Georgina—and I are expected to mingle and make my parents look good. For Claire, the oldest at twenty-six, that means plugging our charities, which she now runs, and pretending it's what she really wants to be doing with her life instead of painting. For Michelle, who's the second oldest at twenty-four and not on good terms with my dad, that means not bursting out in demonic tongue when anyone mentions his name. For little

Georgina, aka Georgie to avoid confusing her with my mother, she's twenty and the youngest of our family. She's also the shyest person on the planet. For her, my parents are just happy if she doesn't end up hiding in a closet. For me, I'm expected to talk football with Dad's guests while being followed around by Candice, the daughter of my dad's longtime friend Big Tom, who's had his mind set on me marrying his daughter since we were ten. My parents agree that it's a good match and insist it's going to happen when I'm done with college.

What do I think?

Ohellno!

Candice is nice enough and actually pretty hot, but I'm not into her. She wants a guy who'll be her second daddy and treat her like a little princess. And if there's anything I can't stand, it's princesses and their three *S*s—spoiled, shallow, and snotty. Candice is so bad that she comes equipped with a forth *S*. Screwy. She actually believes we're getting married.

Never going to happen. I've said so a thousand times, but they're all cut from the same damned stupid-stubborn tree. My father takes the cake, though. "The road to success, Henry, is paved with persistence, pressure, and time," he always says. He thinks I'm like drilling for oil, and if he pushes hard enough, eventually he'll win. It's the same thing with football. "Football is a waste of hardworking energy, Henry. And someday you'll see I'm right."

Of course, when we're in front of his big banker friends who love the sport, my father is all pats on the back. "My boy is quite the player. Couldn't be prouder." Really, though? My father is just waiting for the opportunity to force me to join the family business. He doesn't quite understand that while the money is important, it's not everything. Football is everything.

"Hey, Georgina, nice dress. Going to milk a cow?" says some guy who looks about my age, standing on the back patio with a few giggling teenaged girls. I think they're friends of Candice's.

Georgina, my baby sister, who has long brown hair and the sweetest, kindest heart of anyone I've ever known, was born with chronic debilitating shyness. She's a borderline mute. Unless you get her alone and she trusts you. Then you learn that she's smart as a whip, funny as hell, and incredibly compassionate. She's just not into people. And parties or short dresses. Which is why she kind of just hangs in the background at these events, trying to be invisible or passing for the help by cleaning up. Drives my mother nuts.

I look at the small group of idiots who are eyeing Georgie's long flowery skirt, snickering away at her lack of fashion sense.

"Dude," I jerk my head at the guy, "how *old* are you?"

The guy's head whips in my direction, and his fake tan instantly melts into a pasty shade of khaki.

Obviously, he hadn't seen me standing behind him, talking to one of my dad's invites who wants me to come to his son's peewee football jamboree thing. Of course, I'd love to—I love teaching kids football—but I'm mid-season and then facing my last semester and finals, so I offered to help out next summer.

"Answer me," I demand.

"Uhhh…nine-nineteen?" he stammers.

"Wanna make it to twenty? Then apologize to my little sister," I snarl.

He slowly turns his head toward my sister, who is now absolutely mortified, nearly in tears, because I've called so much attention to her.

Dammit. But what was I going to do, let them make fun of her?

Just as the idiot is about to speak, Georgie bolts inside.

"Excuse me," I say to my father's guest and go after her. I weave through the crowd inside mostly rich people wearing expensive suits and flashy dresses, getting hammered on expensive champagne—and head upstairs to my sister's room. She lives on campus at an all-girls university just outside of Houston, but we all have rooms here for show. Yes, we're one big happy family.

"Knock, knock," I say, poking my head through the door. Georgina is stretched out across her bed, lying on her back with her eyes closed and hands folded across her stomach like a corpse. It disturbs me since the room is so sterile—white carpets, furniture, and linens—that it almost looks like a funeral home. I can't stand thinking about anything ever happening to my sisters. Especially little Georgie.

"Hey, you all right?" I ask.

She doesn't answer.

"I'm really sorry about what happened down there. It just really pisses me off when—"

I notice her lips starting to curve into a muted smile.

"Georgie…" I snarl.

She pops open one green eye and snickers. "Sorry, but I couldn't pass on the opportunity to ditch the party."

"You sneaky little girl."

She sits up. "Who are you calling little? I'm turning twenty-one soon."

I'm only twenty-two, but still, "You'll always be a little brat to me." I sit beside her on the bed and push her face, making her fall back.

"Hey!" She laughs.

"That's what you get for worrying me."

She gets upright again and sits with her legs crossed. "So what's going on with you lately? Why haven't you called?"

"You hate talking on the phone," I point out.

"True. But you could at least call so I know you're still alive or not locked up in the looney bin. I worry."

"Why?"

"I've seen how you're playing lately. I can only assume that the 'roids are getting to you."

I laugh. She knows I don't touch that stuff. Never will. "Nope. I'm still a naturally fucked-up asshole."

"Then what's the deal? I've never seen you suck so badly at football. And I could swear Dad has a perma-smile."

"He tastes blood," I say, debating if I should tell her about the issue that's bringing my father closer to his dream: my football career ending. Hell, maybe I should confess. Georgie will say my head's up my ass and maybe I'll believe her and move on from all this.

"I met a girl," I say.

Her eyes pop wide open. "You're in love?"

"No. It's not like that." I grumble out a breath and rub the back of my neck. "I think she's messed with my...hcadorsomethingreallystupid," I mumble those last words, unable to believe I'm saying them aloud.

"Sorry? What was that? Sounded like you said she's stupid."

I groan. "No, I'm stupid. We only dated casually for a few weeks."

"And?"

"And then she dumped me," I confess, noting how it hurts way more to say than I'd thought.

Georgie's mouth pops open, matching her wide

eyes. "*You* got dumped?"

"Shut up."

"No, sorry, it's just hard to believe." She shakes her head.

I know. I'm awesome. Only, maybe that's changing.

"Well," she continues, "then it makes perfect sense. She's disrupted your game mojo."

"Why? It's not like I got attached to her."

"Maybe not, but you liked her and she dumped you. That's never happened."

"I feel fine. I promise, no broken hearts here." Though maybe I do miss hearing Elle's snorty laugh.

"If you say so, but she's planted a seed of doubt in that thick skull of yours. So you're going to have to find a way to fix it."

But how? Elle hates me. And we fight every time we see each other. "Easier said than done."

"Not really. Whatever you did to piss her off, just apologize."

"I didn't do anything. She says we're just not right for each other and accuses me—*me* of all people—of not being a man."

My sister frowns and rubs her pointed little chin. "Hmmm…then man up. Show her you're not afraid to grovel a little. If that doesn't work, then hit her with the old Henry charm. I've yet to see a girl resist you when you act like an actual human being."

"Gee. Thanks, Georgie," I scoff.

"Call it like I see it." She shrugs. "But hopefully the worst case is you'll end up friends, and it might be enough to let you move on, get your head back in the game."

I start thinking about landing in the friend zone with Elle. I don't like it one little bit. Seems...wrong somehow. On the other hand, maybe I could convince her to come to a few games and test out my theory. Because there's no denying the truth: The moment we stopped seeing each other, my game went to shit. She shows up? Gold again.

Still, I don't have time to dick around, groveling and praying Elle might forgive me. I need to take immediate action.

I look at my sister. "I have to go and check some stuff out. You'll be okay up here by yourself?"

"Way better than downstairs with all those scary people."

My poor sister. One of these days, I'm going to have to figure out a way to get her out of her shell. Some serious social immersion therapy or something. Because sooner or later, she's going to graduate and have to get a job whether it's with my dad or someone else. There are no free rides in the Walton family despite our billions.

I pat her head of brown hair. "Love you."

"Love you, too, Henry." She smiles when she says it, but looks away. It's the one thing we have in common. At the end of the day, we're both kind of private people, and we don't feel comfortable with I love yous. Not even to the people we love. But little Georgie is always my exception.

I get up from the bed and head for "my room" to do some research on my phone and make a call. I quickly find what I need online and then dial Hunter and tell him what I'm thinking.

"Tassie's roomie Elle? Dead-cat T-shirt Elle?" He coughs.

"Yes. Elle," I growl.

"The woman you screwed for a couple of weeks has single-handedly ruined a lifetime of training and now you need her to win," he says with a hint of laughter. "You're not suffering from a concussion, are you?"

Now I'm kind of kicking myself for telling him, but it had to be done. "I'm not the only player who believes in good luck charms. Not that I'm superstitious." Although, if I were, I can't see the big deal. Over eighty percent of our teammates have a ritual or lucky rabbit's foot, so to speak.

"You're really going to tell her all this?" he asks.

"No choice, which is why I need a favor."

"What?" Hunter asks.

"I need you to talk to Tass."

"Why?" he asks.

"Because when I tell Elle, she's going to laugh in my face, accuse me of being illogical and unscientific, and then rip out my nut sack for wasting her time with something so beneath her intellect. Tass needs to convince her to do this."

"Why would Tass do that?"

"Because she's into you, man. She'll do anything for you."

There's a long pause on the other end of the phone, and I'm guessing it's because Hunter just made up with Tass earlier this week after some front-yard, family-versus-family blowout. I know this because yesterday I invited him to the party and he told me about it—the nondramatic version for guys. Anyway, I'm glad it all worked out, because Hunter and Tassie are clearly into each other, unlike me and Elle. I liked her, sure, but I never loved her. Now I just need to find out if my theory is true.

"I don't know, Henry. I'm wondering if Tassie won't throw up on your idea, too."

"Hunter, man, you have to help me." And I know he will because A) he's a good guy and B) I gave him a place to live so he could afford to stay in school and play football since his scholarship only covers the basics and none of us can realistically work during the season. Between practice, games, travel, and classes, we barely have time to study or sleep.

I continue, "Look, man, I know how lame I sound right now. Even telling you this makes my balls want to shrivel up and fall off. But I'm out of options and I'm out of time."

Hunter groans on the other end of the phone.

"I'll talk to Tass, but no guarantees. Our truce is on thin ice. When are you going to do your pitch to Elle?"

"Tomorrow. I'm going to her house."

"On Thanksgiving. Uninvited." His tone indicates he doesn't think that's such a great idea.

"I'm not going to crash their dinner. I'm just going to stop by, beg, and leave. It'll be harder for her to say no on a day when you're supposed to be all charitable."

"How do you know she'll even be home?" he asks.

"I just checked the math tutoring site. She posts her hours and schedule there." Elle once told me to use it so we could figure out our hookup schedule. "Says she's home for the week, but available for online tutoring sessions."

"Stalker." Hunter laughs.

"I call it smart. I'm a resourceful guy."

"I call you fucking nuts, bro."

"Yeah. But what do I have to lose?" I say.

Hunter is silent for once. He gets how far I'm willing to go to succeed. I've told him about my dad.

"I'll call you tomorrow to check in," I say. "And have a happy Thanksgiving with your new in-laws."

Hunter laughs. "Hey, we're not married. Yet. But I am thinking Christmas will be a good time to pop the question."

Huh? Hunter is nineteen, three years younger

than me, so marriage sounds pretty insane. "You're serious."

"Yeah, man," Hunter says without shame. "I mean, we wouldn't get married until after college, but it took us over a decade to get here. Tass needs to know I'm not letting her go."

Oh boy. I sense we're going to need a bigger apartment for next semester—me, Tass, Hunter, Mike C., and Nathan—luckily, my family owns the building. The only catch is my father will want something in exchange. He always wants something. Just getting the apartment in the first place cost me the summer. I'll be working for him, overseeing some new pharmaceutical venture he says is a big moneymaker. I don't mind earning my keep, but I know it's my dad's way of covertly preparing me for what he feels is the inevitable: me giving up on football to work for him. It's why he's forced all four of his kids to major in business. One by one, he guilted us to drop our chosen majors. I'd wanted to get my BA in sports science, focusing on sports management. I thought that maybe someday, when I retire, I might want to have my own agency or something. Too many slick sharks in the sports waters, trying to take advantage of young, bright-eyed athletes looking to get signed. I would protect them and mentor them along the way. Of course, I have to get through my own shark-infested waters first, and there will be no swimming if I don't play with perfection over the next four weeks.

I clear my throat. "Well, thanks for helping me out, Hunt. And I'm glad things are in a good place with Tass. She's, uhh…"

"Overbearing, opinionated, and quirky?" Hunter says.

"I was going to say pretty—but yeah."

"Well, she keeps me on my toes and has since kindergarten. Wouldn't have it any other way."

I think it's a weird match, like if Elle and I decided to get married and have kids. Nerds and jocks just don't make good teams. No common ground when it comes to interests. But hey, maybe Hunter and Tass will be the exception.

"All right," I say. "Call you tomorrow after I visit Queen Brainiac."

"Be careful. I have a feeling she bites."

CHAPTER FOUR
ELLE

I have received seven texts from Henry since yesterday, which is mighty peculiar considering how things ended after his practice last Friday. But I put the blame on myself, of course. I never should have gone to see him, and clearly I wasn't welcome.

Oh, but now you need to talk, Henry? And it's important? I can't imagine what his issue is. Maybe he's lost his jockstrap and his tiny brain needs help finding it. Or maybe they're out of Bud Light for his Thanksgiving feast and he's hoping I know how to make more. I don't know, and I don't care, so I block his number. I don't have time for his juvenile games right now, because from the moment I walked through the front door of my parents' house last Saturday, my worst nightmares came true. My older sister, Lana—who looks like me with blonde hair and brown eyes—was in the living room, consoling Aunt Debbie, my mother's sister. Uncle Frank was nowhere to be found—coward. My father was in the garage, crying over Christmas ornaments. Cousin Keri was keeping my mother company with a box of tissues and her own tears while my mother mustered a smile from her bed and tried to assure her that come what may, it will all be fine.

"Hi, I'm home," I said, peeking into the doorway of my parents' bedroom. "Can I get you anything?"

"Elle." My mother smiled, the circles under her brown eyes darker than the last time I saw her a week ago. "I'm so glad you're home. Maybe you and Keri can make the shopping list for Thursday while I take my nap?" My mother's eyes made a little flicker toward my cousin in a silent plea to get her out of there.

"Sure. Come on, Keri. We'll take inventory of the pantry first."

Keri, who has short black hair and dark eyes and looks more like her dad, Uncle Frank, made a little sniffle. "Okay. But if you need me, just call," she said to my mom.

I wanted to kick her. *Yeah, just what my mom needs, you crying all over her like it's her funeral.* Not that I didn't want to bawl my eyes out, too, trust me, but our jobs were to put on smiling faces and give that woman a happy *fucking* Thanksgiving.

Anyway, after that, I'd gone up to my room to unpack, taking extra care to hang my T-shirts and plan out which ones I'd wear throughout the week. I know how ridiculous some people think the pooping glittery unicorns or historical figures riding dinosaurs look, but they help remind me to smile once in a while. Even the late Mr. Nucleus's sweet little furry face reminds me of better times—the way he used to chase after my laser pointer was pure comedy.

Unlike today. Which will forever be cemented in my mind as the last turkey I'll ever share with my mother. *Fucking, fuck you, cancer.*

My chin quivering and cheeks wet, I check my messages as a distraction. Tass went home last weekend, too, and we haven't had a chance to talk. Apparently, from what I gathered from her texts, the moment she pulled into her parents' driveway, she had some sort of run-in with Hunter, whose parents live next door. "*I hate him! I hate him! I hate him!*" Tass had messaged without any further detail despite my inquiries. Then the next morning I got another text saying, "*I love him! I love him! I love him!*" I seriously hope it means those two have worked out their shit because they're obviously not keen to live without one another despite Hunter being a serious football player and her being a super-nerd, like me.

Yes, I see the parallels to Henry and myself, but those comparative lines are razor thin. Henry and I have only known each other for a few months. He's also rich, hot, and completely closed off. Or self-absorbed.

Ugh. Why can't I stop thinking about him?

Anyway, no new texts from Tass, and it's time for me to get on with my day and help in the kitchen.

I get up from my bed that has my favorite psychedelic cats comforter and go to my old white vanity. It still has pictures of Spock and Princess Leia superglued to it from when I was in high school—at thirteen. I should clean it all off, but I just don't care about any of it.

I look at my puffy face. "Jesus, Elle. You look like crap." My brown eyes are bloodshot, my pale face is ruddy, and my hair looks like it's in dire need of life support. I know I've showered this week, but I can't remember conditioning my hair.

I pick up my brush from my vanity and get to work, making myself presentable for my mother. She needs to see me happy. She needs to see I'm okay.

But I'm not okay. I'm fucking just not.

HENRY

Elle never told me where she lives, but I had no problem finding her address on the Internet. Her house is about an hour away in Bellville—a small town somewhere between Houston and Austin.

My plan is to show up, give her a dozen white roses to call a truce, grovel a little over our last encounter, and then spring my plan on her. I'm hoping she won't yell at me or do that little thing with her lips where she puckers them tightly. A pissed Elle is a scary Elle. She looks like a woman on the verge of a felony, secretly planning your demise. Yes, be afraid of smart women. *Be very afraid.*

Anyway, I don't need to be at my parents' house today because Thanksgiving is always leftovers, hangovers, thank-you calls, counting donations, and—if you're my mother—gossip with your friend about your other friends day. So after this, I'm heading over to Michelle's to hang out with her, Georgie, Claire, and Michelle's new husband, Chukwuemeka-something. I can't remember how to pronounce his name properly, but luckily he goes by Chewy. Michelle met him while on a business trip to Nigeria, and next week they're leaving to spend the holidays with his parents, who are schoolteachers from a small village. I'm fairly sure the trip is because my sister is not on good terms with my parents, who weren't happy about the "scandalous" elopement. Not because they're racist, but because they think any event in our lives should be their opportunity to impress their friends. Especially my mom, who comes from a long line of Coppolas, who are, according to her, Texan royalty because her great-grandfather was one of the first to strike black gold in 1903. Really, they're Italian immigrants who got lucky, not royalty. Anyway, she married my dad, Chester Walton—the son of a banker—and now my dad runs the oil show. He might act like a big important man, but like the old saying goes, "Behind every great man is a powerful woman with a huge inheritance." In any case, I'm definitely eloping, too, if that day ever comes.

I park my car—a black Cadillac SUV because I'm a big guy who likes his comfort and needs his space—in front of the blue, two-story ranch-style house. A jungle of weeds covers the front yard, the windows are dirty, and the roof is mossy.

If it wasn't for Elle's white Nissan Cube in the driveway, I would've thought this run-down place belonged to someone else. She comes across as being from an educated, upper-middle-class family—okay, what I mean to say is she can be a little snobby. *Well, now she's your ticket to success. Go get 'em, tiger!*

I hop from my car, grab my flowers, check myself in the side mirror and smile. I give my blond hair a tousle. It's a mess, just the way I like it. With my jeans and snug black sweater, I pass for presentable. Not too casual. Formal enough to show up at someone's door on Thanksgiving.

I push the weathered, cracking doorbell and straighten my shoulders. With my luck, her dad's going to answer, so I don't want to look like some fuckwad perv stalking his daughter. Besides, if anyone's the perv, it's Elle. Also, just the way I like it.

Dirty, dirty nerd girl… The things she did to me.

Dude, stop. She doesn't like you anymore. This will be purely an arrangement.

One minute goes by. Then another.

Crap. Did I mess up? Are they even home? I wait another moment and then ring one more time. I'd call Elle on her cell, but she's blocked me. I know this because she hasn't answered one call or text. I hate that she's done that. It makes me feel like she thinks I'm shit, not even worth talking to.

"Hello?" A young woman answers the door, and I immediately suspect she's Elle's sister. They have the same color blonde hair, same brown eyes, and same pouty little lips.

"Is Elle here?" I ask, catching a whiff of delicious roasting turkey and spices wafting from inside, making my stomach grumble. I love to eat, but I'm on a strict diet during the season. That means no pie, no mashed potatoes. Just lean meat and whole grains. Okay, and beer once a week. Gotta live.

The woman's eyes nearly pop from her head. "Uhhh…who should I say is looking for her?"

"I'm Henry, a friend. I was just in the neighborhood and decided to stop by," I lie. "You must be her sister. I'd recognize that smile anywhere." After all, it comes with a gap between the two front teeth, kind of like a cute bunny.

Her eyes wash over me—up down, up down, up down. I'm guessing she's wondering what a big handsome man like me is doing on her porch, looking for her little sister.

She gives me a hesitant nod. "I think Elle is up in her room, reading. But come in." She steps aside and lets me in.

I immediately hear lots of voices coming from what looks like the kitchen, through the doorway on the other side of the living room. I also notice how the inside doesn't match the outside. The white tile floor is spotless, and there's zero clutter or dust on the antique furniture in the living room. The couches are covered with white sheets and there are several air purifiers running.

Allergies much?

"Wait here. I'll be right back," Elle's sister says and goes for the stairs.

"Who are you?" asks a man appearing in the hallway ahead. He's got silver, thinning hair, and is wearing thick glasses. He also has on a T-shirt of a turkey dressed like a cowboy that says "Make my Gobble-Gobble Day." This has to be Elle's dad; I can see the resemblance in the eyes and fashion sense.

"I'm Henry. Just stopping by to see Elle for a sec. Happy Thanksgiving, sir."

His eyes set on the flowers in my hand. "Those for Elle?"

I'm instantly happy that I didn't bring red roses, which would only make this moment more awkward. Because nothing says "I want to bang your daughter" like red roses.

"Yeah, I, uh…I sort of insulted her last week and just wanted to say I'm sorry."

He lifts a silvery brow. "You one of her pupils?"

More like she was my pupil of hot orgasms and— fuck. What's wrong with me? So wrong to think that.

"Yes. She's my tutor," I lie.

"Wait! I know you. You're, you're..." He shakes his finger at me.

"Henry Walton."

"Booya!" Her dad claps his hands. "I knew I recognized you. Best defense in the last decade to come out of the college draft."

Hey now. Don't you mean best defense ever?
"Yeah. That's me."

"Wow. Just wow." He shakes his head and then goes all Bambi-eyed on me. "You have to meet my wife. She'll be speechless. Darla! Darla!" he calls out over his shoulder. "You'll never guess who's standing in our living room."

Oh no. This is not what I wanted. My plan was to be covert and slip under the radar, just like the spies in those novels that Elle loves to read.

"Oh, uh...I can't stay," I say. "Really, I just stopped by to give this to—"

"Nonsense. You're not leaving here until you say hi to my wife. She can use something cheery." He grabs my arm and pulls me down the hallway. "Honey, meet Henry Walton! The defensive end for the Pirates."

I step through the bedroom doorway, and what I see makes my heart drop right to the floor. *Fuck, Elle. Why didn't you tell me?*

ELLE

After a long, gloomy morning helping my sister and aunt get started with tonight's dinner, I've retreated to my room to regenerate. I'm knee-deep in the pages of a hot love scene between a Mr. Rook and a guest on his secret sexy island when my sister taps on the door.

Dammit! He was just about to put it in.

"What?" I bark.

The door cracks open, and Lana's blonde bob pops through. She's smiling, but it's not a happy smile. It's the smile she shows when she's gleefully about to watch me suffer—kind of like when your older sibling dangles a loogie over your face while pinning you to the floor.

"Someone's downstairs to see you." She teasingly sings her words.

"Who?" I don't have that many friends, mostly because I was four to five years younger than everyone I went to school with. While they were busy trying to get laid, smoking pot, and thinking about escaping their parents, I was getting braces, figuring out how to use tampons, and studying neutrino oscillation.

Lana wiggles her golden brows. "Never seen the guy before, but he's hot. Like, melts your womanly ice-cream cone from a mile away hot. Or makes you want to climb him like sexual monkey bars and ride his tire swing all day kinda hot."

I can swear she's just gone into full ovulation mode, busting out an egg. Maybe two. It's no wonder she's still single. Desperation is not an aphrodisiac.

She goes on, "Oh, and I just heard dad flip out. So I think they know each other."

Weird. Maybe it's someone from my parents' church. I haven't gone for years, but my dad still attends every blue moon, and there are a few guys my parents have tried to hook me up with.

"I'm busy," I say, but really I just gotta know if Mr. Rook pounds the heroine into the next hemisphere. *God, this book is so naughty.* "And tell Dad I'm not interested in meeting one of his bible buddy's nerdy sons." *Unless they're repressed billionaire monks.*

"Well, this guy is no nerd. And I think he said his name is Henry. But hey, if you don't want him, I'm more than happy to take him off your hands."

Henry?

I spring from my bed. "What! Why is *he* here?"

No, no, no. He can't be here. He can't be inside the bubble. Physics tells us that within the dimensions of space and time exists alternate planes. I have two. Here and school. The worlds must never touch. Their separation keeps me sane. I only allow sunlight and air and things that keep me afloat to permeate the membrane separating my cosmoses. Tass, for example, who I have grown to love like a sister in a few short months, has never passed the barrier physically. She's only passed mentally. Meaning, I have told her about my mother, but she's never been invited inside my other bubble. But now Henry is here, and he's about as welcome as a three-headed Martian with syphilis. Okay, yeah. I watch too much sci-fi. So what?

My heart starts pounding and I don't know whether to panic or be furious or what.

Furious! Definitely furious!

I sidestep Lana, jerk open my bedroom door, and march downstairs. Laughter fills the air the moment my bare feet hit the landing. The sound is coming from the hallway.

"Whatthehell?" *He's in my mom's room?*

Involuntarily, my hands ball into tight fists. "I'm going to kill him."

I stomp my way toward the sound of their little party, and though I have no clue what I'm going to say, I know it will sound something like "Hey! You two-dimensional, freakishly tall ogre. Get out of my house and go back to your stank pond!" But the moment I turn the corner, all thoughts vaporize from my cranium.

My mother is sitting up in her bed, her cheeks are rosy, and she's got the biggest smile on her face. My father is laughing, and Henry's standing there waving his arms around.

"And then," Henry says, "the guy just looks at me and falls over!"

The three of them bust up, and from the corner of his eye, Henry notices me standing there.

"Elle. Hey!" Henry greets me like we're best buds.

"What are you doing here?" I say with a level tone, desperate not to ruin the mood. My mother, for a few short moments, has forgotten her pain.

"Oh, uh," Henry holds out a bundle of white roses, "I came to give you these. Was just in the neighborhood."

Liar. Liar. Jockstrap on fire. "Really now?"

"Well, yeah. And I also feel like I owe you an apology for the way I behaved last Friday." He gives the flowers a little jiggle, urging me to take them.

What's he up to? He's acting all kiss up.

I slowly reach for his offering, my eyes locked on his. "Can we talk outside for a moment?"

"Sure."

"Henry," says my dad, glowing with a full-on man crush, "I know you said you have plans for dinner tonight, but we'd love for you to come back in a few days for our famous turkey potpies. We make them every year."

"Thank you, sir. I'd love that," Henry flashes one of his panty-dropper, dimply smiles, and I'm fairly sure my father's tightie whities are at serious risk of hitting the floor.

Snarl. "Henry? Now?" I set the flowers at the foot of my mom's bed and then turn to leave, beelining for the front door.

I hear Henry's large thumping footsteps trail behind me across the hardwood floor.

It's chilly and overcast outside for once, so I grab a white sweater from the hook by the front door to go over my "Who you callin' turkey?" T-shirt. I then head out and go straight to Henry's black SUV parked curbside, stopping at the driver's side door. Because that is exactly where he's going—in his car and away from here.

I turn and cross my arms over my chest, getting ready to tear him a new one.

Henry's smile evaporates into the atmosphere. "Elle, before you say anything—"

"How. Dare. You," I seethe. "How dare you show up here uninvited and come into my home and invade my—"

"Wait right there." He cuts me off with a tone somewhere between concerned and pious. "Why did you hide your mother's illness?"

"Excuuuuse me? Did you just chastise me for not telling you about my personal business?"

He folds his bulky arms over his chest, mirroring my pose, and lifts his chin. "Yeah. I guess I did."

I open my mouth, snap it shut, and then flap it a few more times. "I—you—how can you—" I fumble my words. "We were sleeping together. I had no obligation to tell you anything."

His despicably gorgeous face turns tomato red. "I thought we were at least friends."

"Wrong."

His lips part like he's about to speak, but he ends up dishing out a long, nice glare.

Finally, he takes a breath and bobs his head. "Well, isn't that nice? I seem to remember you getting all pissed off because I said I wasn't ready to get serious. Only, all the while, you were using me. I was nothing more than a piece of meat to you."

"Oh, get over it. We used each other. And where do you get off making this about you?" He has no idea the damage he's just done to my life. There's a reason I never told him about my mother or anything having to do with my past. I need two worlds, and the happier world needs a happier Elle. The real Elle can't survive in the college universe with normal people talking about normal things and planning out their happy normal lives. I'm not normal. I'm so different that I might be my own species, but that's *my* burden and *my* business. Not his.

"Wrong, princess. This is definitely not about me. It's about *you*. You and your obvious biases. You think because I'm into football that I'm incapable of being a good friend or understanding you or what you're going through."

Damned straight. Henry grew up fitting in and being handsome, rich, and athletic. He possesses zero ability to comprehend me or my situation or my struggles. I literally had to run away after high school, at the age of thirteen, in order to save myself from grown-ups who just wanted to bend me to their will. I have had to fight every step of the way for the right to live my life in my own way. He's had everything handed to him. Everything.

"You know what?" I say. "I can't do this right now. I have real-world issues, something you wouldn't understand, so time for you to go."

"You have no clue what issues I've faced. But you've proved my point, Miss Judgy."

I glare into those pretty green eyes, wondering if I punched one of them, how purple I could make it. My hand is pretty small, so with the right amount of exertion, I could give him a shiner to remember.

That'll teach him never to come here again. Wait. Now that I think about it...

"Henry, why are you here?"

His red face turns sort of pale and then he shrugs and looks at the ground.

"Henry," I warn, but it does no good. I'm left standing there for almost a full awkward minute.

"Fine," I say, "but don't ever come here again. This is my life, and I get to decide who's in it. You're not welcome. You never were."

His head snaps up, and his eyes narrow. "How can you be so cruel, Elle?"

"That's life. What, hasn't anyone told you? Oh, I forgot. You're Henry Walton. Mr. Awesome Football Star."

"You're unbelievable," he snarls. "First you get all upset because I wanted to let our relationship progress naturally, and I was honest about it. Then you dump me and say I'm not serious enough for you, that I'm not a man. But now I realize you were never going to give me a chance. You wrote me off from the moment we met. And now *you* don't want to ever see *me* again? Because I've found out about your mother? You've been nothing but dishonest with me, Elle. But I've been honest with you and completely open-minded. So if anyone should be pissed off, it's me. Not you!"

How dare he yell at me? Where does he get off?

"You want to know why I never told you about my mother?" I say. "Because she's dying, Henry. Fucking dying. A slow, painful, excruciating process, and I don't want your pity. But most of all, I don't want to have to think about it. I don't want to have to look at your stupid beautiful face and see you feeling all sorry for me when what I need is a place where I can pretend that none of this exists. Because here in this world, there is no hope. There is no math equation to save her. There's just my *fucking* misery and my father's *fucking* misery and everyone standing around waiting for her to die, and I can't *fucking* stand it one more *fucking* goddamned minute!"

"Elle?" My father's voice hits me from a few feet away, and I instantly know that I've just shared some horrible things that I shouldn't have said out loud. Maybe I meant some of them; maybe I didn't. The only thing I know is that I'm angry and hurting, and saying these words has only made it worse, especially because my dad is looking at me with tears in his big brown eyes.

"Dad, I'm sorry. I didn't see you there and—"

His face turns from a teary-eyed shock to enraged. "Don't you ever," my dad shakes his finger at me, "say that there is no hope. There is always hope, Elle. Always." I can tell by his tone that I have wounded him in the deepest, profoundest of ways. But can't he see what's happening here? We're all pretending, too. No one is facing the truth about this situation, and we're all bottling it up, feeling like we're all slowly dying with her.

"No, Dad," I say with the quietest of breaths. "There isn't any hope. I've looked at the data a thousand times. The math isn't on her side." He has to face the truth because she doesn't have much time and it's going to kill him when she leaves us if he's not prepared.

"Go," he growls. "And don't come back until you're ready to apologize and change your mind. God forbid your mother—who's fighting for her goddamned life—ever hears you talk like that." He points to my car in the driveway. "Now, go!"

He turns and disappears inside the house, and I feel my insides crumbling. I feel my heart caving in.

Fucking hell. I shouldn't have said that. I shouldn't have said that.

"Elle? You okay?" Henry asks.

I look up at him and his face instantly fills me with bitter rage. "No! I'm not okay, Henry! Look

what you fucking did! And this is her last Thanksgiving. I won't ever get another one with her. Not
ever! Just leave. I don't ever want to see you again."

"But I didn't mean to—"

"I don't care. Go." I head inside to grab my
purse and car keys. By the time I come outside
again, Henry is pulling away in his SUV.

"Happy Thanksgiving, asshole!" I yell, holding
up two middle fingers. "I hope a flock of turkeys
gang-rapes your skull and gives you turkey-cum
stuffing in your ear!"

From the corner of my eye I see two small girls
in pink frilly dresses staring at me. Their mother
and father are just a few yards down the sidewalk.

Oh crap. It's our next-door neighbors, the
Rodríguezes.

I make a little awkward wave. "Sorry. Family
gatherings kind of get to me."

They head inside their house, looking not at all
pleased.

"I'm sorry!" I call out as they close their front
door. "Fuck," I whisper, covering my face and
blowing out a long breath. I've screwed up. I've
really screwed up. And I'm talking about the things
I just said about my mother. Because even someone
as socially challenged as me knows that the truth
isn't always the best policy. Worst of all, I've hurt
my poor father, who's already in so much pain. And
my mother is going to be so heartbroken that I'm
not at the table to eat with them.

An image of her sickly face—with hollow cheeks and eyes—hits me and I begin to cry.

I have nowhere to go except back to the dorms. Alone. On Thanksgiving.

HENRY

"Jesus. What a fucking cluster." If that situation at Elle's had gone any farther south, I'd be licking penguin nuts. *'Cause you just can't get any farther south than that.*

I hit the speaker button on my car's console and tell Sheila (aka Siri, who's been set up as a chick with an Australian accent) to call Hunter. The call goes right into his voice mail.

"Fuck! Fuck!" I pound my hands on the steering wheel and leave a message telling him that I'm an asshole, and therefore, he should call me back simply to agree with my sorry ass.

I then try Elle but, of course, she doesn't answer, and I opt not to leave a message. She's still blocking my number, and I don't know what to say anyway. *Errr...sorry I showed up and ruined your last Thanksgiving with your dying mother? Oh, and by the way...wanna come hang out at my next two games so I can see if you're the reason my playing rocked. Then sucked. Then rocked again?*

I somehow think that won't go over too well, and suddenly my own needs feel diminished. I mean, yeah, I still care about football, but there's this part of me—and it's big—that can't help noticing how what happened back there has genuinely shaken my foundation. All the times I was with her, she was hiding this major thing in her life. She never let on that she felt worried or sad.

Or maybe you're a self-centered douche and never took the time to notice?

I shake my head, shrugging off my lame insecurities, and hit the freeway. What does it matter now? Elle and I are over. And there's no way in hell she's going to help me. And, frankly, I'm pissed. I'm pissed she wrote me off like some...superficial douchebag.

I suddenly begin to wonder if I can honestly blame her. Did I give her a reason to think anything else? We screwed. We laughed. We clicked. But I never really treated her like more than a fling.

My mind starts churning with memories, playing them like an old game reel. I can see me and Elle sitting in my room, laughing as she tries to teach me Klingon. It was the first time I can ever remember just hanging out with a girl and not wanting to be anywhere else. Then there was the time she fell asleep in my arms when I got carried away talking about a game against Alabama. I remember just lying there, staring at her face—the little golden brown eyelashes and soft pink lips. I remember feeling lucky to have her.

I squeeze the steering wheel and grunt out a

breath. Okay. Maybe there was more to us than I realized. Otherwise, why would I be so…so…fucking pissed that she only saw me as fuck material? On the other hand, I never really gave her a chance either. And now, now that I know what was holding her back, I want to. I want to know if she really means more to me than just a football vitamin.

Okay, Henry, I say to myself. *You're not afraid of a little challenge.* And now the goal is clear. A do-over with Elle. Because frankly, my life hasn't felt solid since she left.

CHAPTER FIVE
ELLE

Thanksgiving Day was a black hole and nothing escaped its vacuous force. Not my emotions, not my family, and not even my friends. I'd ended up stopping by the dorms, convinced I could ride out the pity-storm alone in my room with a good book. But there was no amount of literature or steamy love scenes on a dirty, sexy island that could stop the crazy train inside my head. It had left the station, Ozzy at the helm, determined to arrive at its destination: truth.

Henry had shattered the fragile barrier separating my two worlds, and then my brain did the rest. I was no longer able to compartmentalize my fears or sorrow, and worst of all, I realized I was a giant hypocrite. I'd told my dad to face the truth, yet I wasn't able or willing to do it myself.

Now the train of truth is moving full steam ahead, barreling over everything in its path. Which was why I'd found myself driving to Tass's house on Thanksgiving evening and collapsing in hysterics in her front yard.

God, what Hunter must think of me. Or Tass's family. Snot had been flying, hiccups exploding, tears gushing. I was a mess. *I think it's called an emotional breakdown, Elle?*

Tass then gave me lots of water, put me in her bed, and curled up with me. The next morning we decamped for the dorms, and I could barely face her family, who, to their credit, just kept hugging me and telling me that it would all be okay.

It won't, of course. But that's my reality to face.

Anyway, it's been five days since I hit the muddy layer of silt lying over rock bottom. The only thing that gives me comfort is knowing I can't sink much lower.

"Hi, Elle!" Tass bolts through the door of our dorm room, which reminds me of a sad gray cloud. No amount of decorating can overcome the stained gray carpets and ugly brown furniture, not even our brightly colored bedding and nerd-girl posters.

"Guess who I just ran into?" She pants her words, like she's run all the way here.

I glance up from my bed, where I'm sitting in my favorite orange PJs with my back against the headboard, my history book propped on my lap. Tass is wearing a Pirates sweatshirt—XL, so I know it's Hunter's—and has her dark curly hair in a ponytail.

"Santa?" I reply. "He's come early and decided to put me out of my misery before Christmas arrives?" I still haven't spoken to my father. I just don't know what to say. Somehow "sorry" doesn't feel adequate.

"Dork!" Tassie snorts. "I saw Henry. In fact, he's standing right outside and wants to know if it's safe to come in and see you."

I huff. He's the last person I ever want to see. "Uhh…that would be a no. Tell the Jolly Mean Giant to shoo."

Tass lifts her dark brows. "Oh, come on. He didn't know about your mom, Elle. At least talk to him—let him grovel a little."

"Nope. I'm good." I pretend to go back to my reading, but really I'm thinking about my pulse. It's going warp speed, and I'm not sure if it's because Henry is standing outside, likely looking his usual hot self, or because Henry is standing outside and I'm mad at him.

"Elle," Tass sits on the edge of my bed, "I think you're making a mistake. You need a little fun in your life right now, and he really seems to like you. At least I assume so since he's standing out in the hallway, holding a giant teddy bear while random people walk by, snickering at him."

A mental image of Henry—big, huge, manly, muscled Henry with a perma-five o'clock shadow—holding a big fuzzy bear pops into my head. I bet he looks kind of cute.

No. He looks desperate.

"Come on, Elle. Give him a chance." Tassie bats

her hopeful blue eyes at me.

"You just want me to date him because now you're dating Hunter and you don't want to go alone to all his football thingys." Hunter is the star quarterback, and it's no secret that his choice to date Tassie will cause a little controversy. She's a diehard nerd like me and is not ashamed to show it. For example, she attended the game yesterday, where Henry did not play. Not that I care. But Tassie was there, wearing a big orange traffic cone on her head. She said that it would make Hunter laugh every time he looked at her, and since laughter is scientifically proven to boost cerebral function and physical stamina, he would play a perfect game. He did.

"Thingys?" she asks. "They're called games, and yes. Selfishly, I'd love to have you there because I like you, but not for any other reason than that. I'm fine hanging out with the Gamma Nus. They're actually lots of fun!"

The Gammas are the cheerleader sorority. Tassie, of all people, made friends with a few of them after discovering they actually have brains and aren't nearly half as snobby as the Kappa Kappa Kappas—the nerd-girl sorority, or as I like to call them, the Sisterhood of Intellectual Nazis because they hate anyone who's not a card-carrying member of Mensa. We almost joined, but then realized we were too socially evolved and didn't appreciate them telling us we couldn't date football players.

Not that I want to. I'm so over Henry.

"Tell him to go," I grumble. "I'm not interested in being his sex toy."

"Actually, that's not quite accurate. You're going to love this." Tassie hops up and bounces over to her own bed to fully face me like it's story time. Her bed is covered with a huge pile of clean clothes she washed over at her parents' last week. Since she's been sleeping over at Hunter's place (which is really Henry's off-campus man-palace that he shares with Hunter and two other guys), she hasn't had the need to fold. I'd talk to her about it, but I've got bigger problems. And it makes it easier for me to steal her clean socks because I haven't had time to wash my own.

She continues, her pale face a bright shade of giddy, "Okay. Ready for this? Because when I heard, I got all gooey inside. It's just *that* adorable."

"What?" I snap, growing impatient.

"It has to do with the real reason Henry came to see you on Thanksgiving. He—" Her cell buzzes in her jeans pocket. "Oh, crap. Sorry. It's my mom. I have to take this." She pulls out the device and answers. "Hey, Mom. What's up?" Tass heads outside to talk, closing the door behind her. Why everyone goes out there to have private conversations is beyond me, but I expect her to return right away, and she doesn't.

Whattheheck? Did she really just leave me hanging like that?

My mind instantly hops, skips and jumps to the

worst possible conclusion. Something's happened. Something bad.

I get up to check the hallway and immediately encounter a furry orange wall blocking my entire doorway.

"Hello there, princess." Henry peeks over the top of the biggest orange teddy bear I've ever seen. With the way he's holding the thing and his height, I feel like I'm being invaded by giant gummy bears.

"Henry," I say, in a snit, "you still here?"

"Yep. And I'm not leaving until we talk."

I shrug. "Sleep outside, then. No skin off my teeth." I close the door in his bear's face and grab my cell from my nightstand to text Tassie.

Me: *What happened? U OK? Pls tell me no one died.*

Sounds like a joke, but it's not. I really hope nobody's hurt, injured, or on life support. I'm hyper paranoid at this stage of my life, and lucky me, my brain is very efficient at throwing out all sorts of possible explanations for her sudden departure. Gas line explosion at her house, tornado, space aliens— *oh, maybe Russians!* Everyone knows how crazy *those* people are.

Tass: *Everything's fine! Forgot a book over in the science lab.*

Huh. But she disappeared after that call with her mom, and it's not like her to cut out on me in the middle of a serious conversation. She had been about to tell me why Henry came to my house last week.

Me: *You sure?*

Tass: *All OK! Be back in a minute.*

Humph! I set down my phone and stare at the ceiling for a moment. My gut tells me she's lying.

Well, logic says that if something happened, I'll find out soon enough.

A knock at the door quickly reminds me that I left Henry outside.

Jesus, buddy! I sigh and walk over, jerking open the door. "Take a hint! I'm not interested."

But there's no Henry. There's just an orange bear propped up against the wall, sitting directly in front of the door.

I stare at its glassy blue goo-goo eyes and silly smile. "Don't look at me like that. You're not coming in." Even if orange is my favorite color, which Henry must've remembered.

The bear mocks me with his unshakable goofiness.

"Fine." I point and shake my finger at him. "But you're only staying until I can find you a suitable home."

I pick the thing up and am immediately hit with the smell of Henry's cologne. I'm suddenly unable to stop myself from burying my nose in the bear's head and inhaling the sweet fresh scent that floods my mind with memories of holding Henry, of him touching me, of us lying in bed, laughing. My heart tightens around a hollowness inside it.

I look down and suddenly realize I'm standing in the middle of the hallway, sniffing a giant teddy bear. *Jesus, what's wrong with me?*

Henry can't change things with a stupid bear. We're two different people. We always will be.

I set the bear back down in the hallway and return to my room.

HENRY

This is not failure. It's just a setback. But like every determined athlete, perseverance is key.

I lean back in my computer chair—XXL and ergonomic, because I'm a big man who likes to take big care of himself—and stare at my computer screen, examining the play.

Yes, for fuck's sake, I've created a game plan for Elle. I find organization is key and planning is essential.

I scratch my stubbled chin and reach for the mouse on my desk, clicking off the box on my screen.

Orange bear is a dud. I've only given a stuffed animal once in my life, and it got me laid. Five times. Five girls. Same time. Same night. That was my freshman year and taught me a valuable lesson:

quality, not quantity. Guys get off on these fantasies of being the big stud, fucking a dozen women at once in an act of pure male showmanship. But unless you were born with twelve cocks, someone is bound to be left out in the cold. Then there's the whole obstacle of most women taking much longer to come, which means that for them there'll be a lot of waiting around. So while men can dream big, there's no glory in going home with only half the job done. Point is, that night was a fail and so was the bear. Both are off the list for good.

I move to the next item on my list, a gem guaranteed to humiliate the hell out of me and convince Elle to forgive me—the first step in our possible reboot.

My finger hesitates on the mouse, urging me to skip this idea. It's really, really going to make me look like an idiot if it doesn't work.

No. Be strong, Henry. This one is a winner. No woman can resist such a powerful public display of affection.

CHAPTER SIX
ELLE

Every Thursday, Tassie and I have a two-hour break in the afternoon between classes, so we've been meeting up to jog around the track since the Texan weather is cooler this time of year. Today, though, she said she wanted to skip the exercise and meet up for coffee over in the common, where everyone hangs out to eat or study or veg. Sounds good to me because the only thing I want is to finish our conversation from Tuesday. The one where she just disappeared midsentence and then never returned. She's been staying over at Hunter's place, which means she's also seen Henry. I won't lie, I do feel a little jealous that she's all snuggled up with a man at night, and I'm left behind in our ode-to-depression dorm room.

Toting my purple backpack, I immediately spot Tass sitting in the center of the indoor space that reminds me of a mall food court with its three-story-high ceiling, mood plants, skylights, and ocean of café tables filled with students. Around the perimeter of the first floor are the various food shacks and a convenience store. On the second and third floors— with catwalks overlooking the table area—are the various student service offices, bookstore, and student group headquarters.

Tass spots me and gives a quick wave followed by a shit-eating grin. *Uh-oh...* That's the sneaky look my sister, Lana, always gives me when she's up to something.

I weave through the clusters of tables and piles of backpacks littering the floor. "All right, what's with the guilty smile?" I plop down in the chair across from her.

"Nothing." She bites the inside of her cheeks.

"You're a terrible liar." So bad, in fact, that I've only known her for three months and I can spot her fibs from five light-years away.

She continues smiling, her eyes watering, but she doesn't speak.

"Ugh. Okay, I don't have time for this." I start getting up from my chair.

"Wait! Okay! I'll tell you, but..." She half-winces, half-smiles.

"But what?" I fold my arms across my chest.

"Well, there are really two parts to this. The first is hard for me to tell you because it's so premature, but on the other hand, it looks so promising, and I feel like if you knew, it might change your bad mood, even if it's for a few short weeks while we wait. I mean, if it doesn't work out, at least you have that and—"

"Tassie, please. Just spit it out."

She shows me her two palms. "Okay, okay. As you know, my mother is very well known in the cancer research arena, and after your visit the other day, she did some poking around."

My heart starts to race. "And?" I unfold my arms and rest them on the metal table.

"And," Tassie reaches out and grabs my hand, "there's a new drug that's just been approved by the FDA. It's an immune booster that's been very effective in treating cancers that don't respond well to chemo or radiation."

My heart starts to accelerate out of control, filling with a rush of hope. I want to pull it back, but I can't help myself. This is a door that's been welded shut for over a year and somehow Tassie's managed to crack it open, allowing a tiny sliver of light to shine through.

"What's the statistical data for her particular condition? What's the relapse rate and average time for treatment validation?"

"Whoa." Still grinning, Tassie throws up a palm again. "All great questions, and my mom is getting the data for herself to review, but that's not the challenge."

"What, then?" Because I would move heaven and earth to save my mom. I would auction off every expendable body part I own to an underground people chop shop, I'd write people's term papers (I hate cheaters, but I'd do it!), and I'd even sign over my brain to the U.S. government—they already asked, but I turned them down.

"The medicine is so new that supply is very limited, and it's definitely not covered by any insurance out there. But they do have a program where they'll give the medicine to a certain number of people each year as part of their legal obligation to continue studying the drug's efficacy."

"Oh." My heart sinks. This means two things: One, getting the drug won't be easy. And two, if my mother did manage to be part of the ongoing study, there's a big chance she'd be part of the control group, meaning she'd get a placebo.

"Elle, don't give up hope. My mother is going to pull every string she can for you." Tass squeezes my hand. "This is good news. It's something to hope for."

I flash a shallow smile. She's right. Of course, I won't tell my mom because there'd be nothing worse than getting her hopes up and this not panning out.

"Please thank your mother," I say. "This is really, really incredible of her to do this. When will we know more?"

"Soon. My mom knows time is of the essence, so she's calling in every favor she can."

I start to get all teary eyed. Her mother doesn't even know me, and for her to go out of her way like this is truly touching. "Thank you. Tell her thank you."

"Elle," Tassie says with a stern tone, "you don't need to thank me. I know you'd do the same if the tables were turned."

I bob my head, staring at our touching hands and thinking about how comforted she makes me feel. I suddenly can't help but wonder if I've made a big mistake by shutting her out before. If I'd opened up sooner and invited her into my real life, maybe we would've found out about this drug months ago. Instead, I kept her at arm's length and made it clear that my mom wasn't a topic open for discussion.

What the hell is the matter with me?

"Thank you," I say. "You're a really good friend."

"Hey, like I said, don't mention it. But you didn't ask about your second surprise."

I don't think anything could get better than the news she's just delivered other than my mother getting the drug and beating this brain tumor.

"You're getting married, and I get to sing karaoke at your wedding?" I reply snarkishly.

Tassie snorts out a laugh and then pushes her glasses up her nose. "Like I'd ever get married. That's, like, dinosaurs and cavemen." She swipes her hand through the air. "Thankfully, Hunter knows how silly I think marriage is. My commitment to be with him is given freely, which is way sexier and much more meaningful compared to a partnership of a legal nature."

"Agreed. So what's the second surprise?" I ask.

"It's that." She jerks her head in the direction over my shoulder.

Suddenly, the cavernous room explodes with strange music.

I turn my head and twist my body to see where this…this noise is coming from. "What. The. Fuck?"

CHAPTER SEVEN
HENRY

Ah…the sweet sound of mariachis. Nothing in this world is more capable of simultaneously embarrassing, flattering, and making a woman laugh than twenty dudes dressed in tight black pants with shiny silver buttons and giant sombreros. And these guys are the best. My parents have booked them for parties dozens of times.

First, I stay behind as the troop of mariachis descends into the common with an explosive version of the only song I know well, "El Cucaracha." I wait twenty seconds for the romantic gesture to work its magic before coming around the corner in my own personal mariachi outfit. I bet no one knows that in addition to being an awesome lover and kick-ass DE, I also play trumpet—my mother demanded we all learn music in elementary school as part of a well-rounded education. Now I'm seeing the logic.

Yes, I am a man of many talents. *Add seduction to the list.*

As I come up behind the wall of flashy black

suits, I see hundreds of students stand, clapping and gathering around. The balconies encircling the massive room are packed with onlookers.

Oh, yeah…. Henry has hit this one out of the piñata park!

I give a quick "go time" nod to the five women standing with me, all wearing bright Mexican floral dresses and carrying red roses. I've already pointed out Elle sitting at a table with Tassie, so they know where to go.

I give my lips a lick and place the tip of my trumpet to my mouth, walking slowly out in front of the musicians. I can't wait to see Elle's face smile, I realize. Because there's really nothing like it. Glowing brown eyes, a sexy little vixen-esque gap between her two front teeth, and honey blonde hair that seems to frame it all up into something that reminds me of my favorite dish. Pasta.

Quickly, I spot the women surrounding Elle's table, dancing in a circle and laying flowers at her feet to spell out "I'm sorry."

Only Elle isn't smiling. In fact, she looks…well, I'm not sure. Pissed maybe?

Oh no. But I can't stop now. I'm committed.

I blow out the final notes of the timeless tribute to roaches and take my place in front of my compadres, getting to my knees and extending my arms. "Elle, will you go out with me again?"

From her seat, Elle begins snarling with those pink lips, and I'm fairly sure I'm going to soil my very, very large mariachi pants. She is so pissed.

I look at her as if to say, "What's the matter?"

She gets up, turns, and leaves the room. I feel my ego deflate like a leaky balloon. This is cringingly painful. Really, really painful.

I look at Tassie, who just stares with pity, as do the other students, who've caught on that this is a romantic gesture gone wrong.

Fuck. How did that not work? I get to my feet and gesture for the music to stop. The musicians look at me with a respectful nod. Apparently, I am not the first guy to get shot down in their presence.

The biggest mariachi, after myself of course, steps forward. "That will be one thousand dollars, *señor.*"

Huh?

I blow out a breath and nod. "Sure. No problem. Just keep playing." At least the entire student body will be entertained for the next forty minutes.

As for me, I'm done. I'm done begging, groveling, and trying. Because if staying in the game means I've got to kiss up to that ice-cold, abominable snow woman, then I give up!

My heart bucks inside my chest, like it's protesting. Of course it is. I'm not a quitter. And giving up now isn't just giving up on Elle, it's giving up on football.

Fuck. What the hell does she want from me?

ELLE

Once outside the common, I double over and start laughing hysterically. I'm not going to lie. Henry has managed to simultaneously flatter and embarrass the hell out of me. But you know that feeling when you're mad at someone and they try to make you laugh by saying something stupid like, "Come on...don't be mad...You gonna make a wittle laugh?" while using baby talk or some other silly voice? Well, that's kind of how I felt. I didn't want to smile and give Henry the satisfaction of thinking he'd won me over.

"Elle! Ohmygod. Are you okay?" Tassie catches up to me on the walkway leading to the dorms and places her hands on my shoulders. "I'm so sorry! Please don't cry. I didn't know it would upset you. I thought it would cheer you up."

I snort a few times, unable to stop myself from laughing. And yes, I am crying, but they're not tears of sadness.

"Elle? Are you...laughing?"

I shake my head and stand upright. "Yes."

She smiles. "Ohthankgod. I thought maybe you had some strange mariachi phobia we didn't know about and we'd triggered you."

"No..." I wipe my eyes with the backs of my hands.

"Then why'd you run away?"

I finally feel my laughter dying down and take a deep breath. "I don't know. I mean, I guess I'm not ready to forgive Henry and I felt like he was shoving it down my throat." I hate pushy people.

Tass nods with a pensive look on her face—brown brows knitted together, puckered lips. "I suppose that makes sense. But you have to admit, he's really trying."

She makes a good point, but I can only wonder... "Why? Why is he trying so hard? He knows we're not compatible."

"Can I be honest? That's not what I saw when you two were together."

I frown, indicating I think she's been smoking something.

"No. Really." She gives my arm a little squeeze. "Remember the weekend when we went to Henry's lake house, before Hunter and I had our blowout?"

Henry's parents have a huge log cabin on Lake Travis about ten times the size of my parents' house. A bunch of us went there for an overnighter, but Tass and Hunter got into a sort of fight, so I left early with her.

"How could I forget?" I say.

"Well, when we got to the cabin and Henry opened the door to greet us, I don't think I've ever felt more jealous than anyone in my entire life. The way his face lit up when he saw you."

Henry had then grabbed me, thrown me over his shoulder like a little doll, and proceeded to tickle me.

"Yeah, well," I rub the back of my neck, "my bladder was full, and he almost made me pee myself."

Tassie smiled. "You were also laughing your ass off, and it's the happiest I've ever seen you."

I hit pause on my bitterness and the negative voice inside my head, allowing Tassie's words to soak in. She's not entirely wrong, but—

"He just cares about partying and football, Tass. How's that supposed to be a good match for someone like me?" She doesn't know what I've been through and how strange and complicated my past is. Henry has this perfect happy life. He'd never understand me.

"I have a theory," she says, "about why I think Henry is a match. I think we can both agree that the universe has an intelligence far superior to our own, which says a lot because you and I are super smart. We're like her little brainy minions. Brainions!" She snorts and I wait for her to finish.

"Oh, sorry," she says. "I think that the universe knows we can't all be going through hell at the same time; otherwise, everyone would be jumping off bridges. Some of us have to be in a good place—a happy place—so we can lift up the people in our lives who are going through a rough spot. And you can't argue that rough spots are simply part of life. As painful as they are, we need them to grow as human beings, and we need them because they help us place a value on the good stuff. But we can't survive those rough spots alone, and it's our friends, family, and Henrys who help us get through it."

I get what she's saying even if there's no scientific data to support it. Nevertheless, "Your theory is sound, but I have to point out that then I'm wasting my time with Henry because I won't be in this place forever, Tass. At least, I hope not." Life has to get better. It has to. "So at some point, years from now, I won't need a party king to make me smile. I'll be thinking about building my future. I can't see building it with him." His dream is to go pro and live in the limelight. My dream is to give free, clean energy to the masses. *Don't forget about building a tele-transporter.* While I'm off in the lab, working twelve hours a day, he'll be surrounded by hordes of eager hot women and thousands of screaming fans. Sooner or later, he'll be wondering why I'm not by his side, cheering with the rest of them. That's what a good woman would do for him, right? But God did not give me this annoyingly powerful brain and make me suffer growing up just so I can sit on the sidelines, watching someone else live their dream.

Tassie sighs and glances at two lovebirds walking past us, hand in hand. "I'm not going to lie. Henry has some growing up to do, but you two have amazing chemistry. And just look how far he's come since he met you, Elle? He told off his entire fraternity after you made him realize how juvenile and disrespectful they were being to women."

She has a point.

"And sooner or later," she adds, "Henry is going to hit his own rough patch, and I think you'll be just the person he needs. Rational, smart, and compassionate. You know how to carry the heaviest of the heavy on your shoulders and keep going. You're the strongest, most determined person I know."

I'm shocked that she gets that about me, because I've never told her about my past, which almost broke me. It's why, after high school, when every university and branch of government was coming at me, making offers and promising the moon, I said no. I felt like everyone wanted to own me and use me, but no one cared about how I felt or that I was only thirteen and had no friends. It's why I ran away to live with my uncle Seymour, who—according to my mother—had been just like me. If anyone could understand what I'd been going through, surely it was the estranged uncle who decided one day to quit his job as a scientist for some big company and live like a leaf, blowing in the wind. Anyway, I'd found his last known address in San Diego on a postcard and went to see him.

"I know what you're going through, kid," he'd said, "but you can't stay. I'm leaving tomorrow—just got a job with the circus."

I'd never heard of anything so illogical and crazy, yet, strangely it appealed to me. I wanted fun and magic. I wanted to be a kid.

"Then take me. Take me with you," I'd begged.

Uncle Seymour had laughed me off. "You're thirteen. You should be in school, enjoying your childhood, Elle."

"They won't let me, and you know why. Please, I'm begging you. There's nowhere else for me to go, and I'm not going back." I felt like my parents just wanted to sell me to the highest bidder.

I remember the conflicted look in my uncle's eyes. He knew what I was going through. Anyway, he'd said yes as long as he could get my parents' approval, which they reluctantly gave once he explained that I'd intended to disappear forever. I think they were afraid that with a brain like mine, I might actually figure out how to make good on my threat. So I joined the circus. My dirty, happy, weird little secret. I was a teenage clown—a story so outrageous that it threatens to be a cliché. Or a Lifetime miniseries. But traveling from town to town with fellow "freaks," meeting people from every walk of life, well, I found myself. But more importantly, I got to be a kid. Yes, I had to work, but I also got to just have fun. Anyway, I ended up staying with my uncle until I was fifteen. Then I came home, thinking I was mentally prepared to start a new chapter of my life: college.

Wrong.

I took one tour of Harvard and almost had a heart attack. I mean, everyone stared at me, especially the guys—full grown men, really—who were all thinking the same thing: "What's with the little girl in big glasses?" I couldn't go through it again— being surrounded by people who made fun of me or saw me as an exhibit at a zoo.

After that, I vowed never to go back to college. My parents were livid. *Livid.* In their minds I was wasting my life. But this time, I didn't run. I stood my ground, endured their lectures, and figured I'd be eighteen in a few years. Meanwhile, I had to prepare for my future. I would educate myself with books and change the world on my own terms.

So, starting at fifteen, I began reading every textbook and lecture from the physics programs at every Ivy League out there, all the way through to the PhD programs.

At seventeen, my mother started getting headaches.

At eighteen my mother was diagnosed with a brain tumor.

At nineteen, they said it was incurable, and she only asked me to do one thing: go to college. Any college. She just needed to know that I would be okay and happy and able to support myself doing something I loved. "At least with a degree, you can get your foot in the door anywhere you go." Meaning, I couldn't just show up at a job interview and show them my IQ score or a list of books I'd read. So that landed me here with Tassie, fulfilling my mother's dying wish, me trying to fit in with all these people, only now the equation has shifted. We all match in age, but I feel like I've lived a lifetime, whereas they're just starting out, still bright eyed and filled with hope. But I'm not like them. I grew up a long time ago. I know that life is fucking hard. And *that* is the point. How could someone like Henry ever possibly "get" me? We'll never be in the same place in life and it hurts to think about it. It's scary to feel so alone in the world. But I like him enough to know that I don't ever want him to be like me. Everyone should be allowed to grow up in their own time, in their own way.

I look at Tassie, my new friend, and know I'll never tell her all this, because it will only make her worry and I want her to be happy.

I clear my throat. "Tass, you're really a great friend. And I really, really appreciate everything you're saying, but—"

"But you're not going to give Henry a chance, are you?"

"No."

She presses her lips firmly together and bobs her head, staring at the ground. "Well, I think you're making a mistake. But okay. If you feel that strongly, then there's no way to change your mind. I'll drop it. And I'll tell Henry to back off."

"Thanks." I offer her a shallow smile.

"Well, I better go back there and check on Henry." Tass points to the common.

I nod.

"He's going to be really bummed, though," she

adds. "Hunter says Henry thinks you're like some lucky charm. He hasn't been playing well since you dumped him, and it's really messed with his head."

I want to laugh, but it's too ridiculous even for that. Jocks and their silly superstitions. So irrational.

"I'm sure he'll find some new inspiration," I say, "like not washing his underwear or performing some lucky masturbatory ritual before every game."

"Ewww…" Tassie laughs. "I hope not. But either way, I think he's out of time. I heard from one of the Gammas that Henry didn't play the last game because he's only got one more chance. If he screws it up, he'll be benched for the rest of the season, which means he's not going pro when he graduates."

I wonder if he didn't play because of me—he didn't have his lucky charm. I don't really know how to feel about that other than kind of sad for him.

"That's awful," I mutter.

"Not as awful as his dad. Hunter says he's just waiting for Henry to fuck up so Henry will be forced to work for him."

Tass's words strike a furious, outraged chord with me. Why does everyone insist on being such assholes? Henry has a right to live his life and be happy. It disgusts me that Henry's father would push Henry to be someone he's not.

I shake my head. "I just don't get people. I really don't. Just makes me want to throw in the towel and go back to tiny cars and balloon animals."

"Huh?"

"Nothing. Never mind. You staying at Hunter's tonight?" I ask to change the subject quickly.

"Yes. But he's taking off tomorrow for a game in Ohio. He won't be back until Saturday night. Wanna hang then?"

"Yes. I could use a quality movie and Hot Pocket night with you," I say. It's been weeks since we've had drama-free hang-out time together.

"Oh! Me too. But I hear they have a *Star Trek* Friday night marathon tomorrow on the second floor of the dorms."

"Oh. Even better. I'll wear my Spock ears."

Tassie claps. "I'll wear my Klingon forehead!"

Her words instantly make me think of Henry and the time I nearly peed myself laughing, trying to teach him Klingon. For the life of him, he couldn't get a single word let alone the phrase "I like smooth foreheads" or "Hab QuchDu' vIparHa'." Henry, though, didn't give up. "I can get this. I can learn to speak your sexy nerd language." He'd laughed.

"Okay. So *Star Trek* marathon in the dorms it is." Tassie gives me a hug I desperately need and then pulls away. "Chin up, Elle. Everything's going to be fine."

I don't know. For the first time in a very long time, I feel like something big is missing from my life. I can't help wondering if it's Henry.

CHAPTER EIGHT

HENRY

This week has not been easy for me. It's been hell, actually. Especially after yesterday's mariachi mishap. But Elle's very public rejection, confirmed by Tassie as being Elle's final no, has made me stop and think. Hard.

Why am I really going through all this? The fact that I'm willing to endure this kind of humiliation for a woman has really put me into thinking mode. I would never let anyone chew me up and spit me out so many times.

Maybe it's my drive to win. Maybe it's more. I really don't know. I just know that I'm done with the gimmicks and I need to see Elle and tell her...

I fucking don't have a clue. The painful mess inside me is new territory, but if I don't come clean and tell her what I think is happening, then I won't just lose my dream. I'll lose her, too, which is unacceptable and completely blows my mind. How can someone you hardly know mean so much?

Anyway, I've decided it doesn't matter and that

I need to make one last play—a Hail Mary—to try to save it all. Because Coach has made himself clear: I've been playing like shit, and I only get one more opportunity to prove myself. One. So while he let me skip the last game, he said I have to show him my stuff tomorrow against Ohio.

"Dude, you ready to hit the road?" Hunter says, standing in the doorway of my room on Friday night, his black Pirates duffel bag slung over his shoulder.

"I have to finish an English paper. It's already late, so if I don't email it to my professor tonight, she'll give me an F." There is no way I can tell Hunter the real reason I'm taking the red-eye to Ohio. He'd shake his head at me and that's something I can't handle. Yeah, normally I don't give a shit what anyone says about me, but I'm stressed to my limit. I've got to turn things around.

Hunter's blue eyes twitch, and I wonder if he knows I'm bullshitting him.

"Yeah," he says. "I guess doing your work on the plane can be a little distracting."

Yep. He knows I'm lying. All the guys do work while we're on the road. There's no other way to keep up if you really intend to graduate, which not everyone does. Some squeak by while they hope they get drafted for the NFL. But the rest of us know that as much as we love the game, we all have a short shelf life. Maybe that's why we all try so hard. This is our time, and once it's over, it's over.

There are no do-overs, no catching the train once it's left the station.

"It's Shakespeare," I lie. "I can't wing it. Besides, I prefer the comfort of my family's private jet over your commercial coach hell any day. Yanno, big muscles and all." I flex a bicep and give my right gun a peck.

"You call those mini marshmallows big?"

"Sure. But you and your wimpy quarterbacking ass wouldn't know anything about being big." I crack a smile.

Hunter fake snarls. "You're a dick."

"Oh, that's big, too. Wanna see?" I reach for the front of my black sweats.

"Already seen it. Wasn't impressed," he throws back. "See you and your tiny cock at warm-up in the morning."

"Yep. Big, bright, and early." I go back to my computer. A few minutes later, I hear the front door close, and I know the coast is clear. My roommates are meeting up with the team bus and heading for the airport. Meanwhile, I've got to prepare myself to do something I've never done before.

ELLE

"Ohmygod." Gripping Tass's arm, we make our way up the stairs after the *Star Trek* marathon, heading for our own floor in the dorms. "I can't remember the last time I laughed so hard." A lie. It was with Henry, but I don't want to think about him anymore.

"I'm pretty sure half the guys there had huge stiffies when I walked into the room," Tass says. "Who knew a bony forehead was such an aphrodisiac?"

Her Klingon costume—really a long dark wig with a forehead mask—had been a huge hit, although the guy sitting next to me kept rubbing my knee with his phaser. But he was a red shirt. No self-respecting sci-fi girl is into wimps who can't even last ten seconds.

"I definitely think a few boxes of tissues will die in your honor tonight," I say to Tass with a chuckle.

"Ewww...Elle!" Tass slaps my arm. "That's gross."

"But so true," I throw back, noting that next time, I'm definitely wearing the Klingon wig.

We *trek* our way up the stairs, and I pull out my key to unlock the door, but the moment I go to insert it, the door pops open. I look up, and standing there is Henry. He's wearing my favorite outfit on him—well, aside from naked.

I look him over in his snug black T-shirt and faded jeans. I love how they show off the contours of his bulky biceps, hard pecs, and tight waist.

I can't lie. Even now, my attraction for him is hard to fight. But I must.

"Hey." He flashes a smile. "Sorry to intrude, but

the door was unlocked, and I didn't want to wait outside."

I lift a brow. "So you just invade my private space like a three-hundred-pound stalker?"

"I weight two eighty, and I'm a perfect gentleman." His green eyes flash to the ceiling then come back to my face. "Okay, except for that time you asked me to bend you over and—"

"Henry…" I growl. "What are you doing here?"

He looks over my shoulder at Tass. "Mind giving us a few minutes?"

"Elle?" she says, making sure I want her to go.

"Sure. It's fine. See you in ten because that's all I'm giving him," I say.

Tass makes a little wave. "See ya, Henry."

"See ya, Tass," he replies and then steps aside so I can enter, closing the door behind me.

I immediately go into defensive mode, crossing my arms. I'm not mad that he's trying, I'm mad because he's making this harder on me than it needs to be. We won't work. I'm trying to do the right thing here.

"Okay, make it quick," I say, "because I meant what I said. I don't want to see you anymore, and you being here means that you don't respect that or you think this is some sort of game. Oh, and yes, I know about your losing streak, and that you think I'm your talisman, which changes nothing. Except that I think you're more ridiculous than ever."

Henry's large body goes all rigid, and I can see

the veins pulsing in the side of his neck. He's pissed.

"All right, Elle. I know you don't want me here, but I won't let you talk to me like that. So before you say one more bitchy little word, you might want to stop and just listen to what I have to say. If that's even possible."

Oh, oh, oh, there's that bitchy word again. Who does this guy think he is? Well, too bad for him, I love a challenge. *So bring it on, big guy.* Because whatever he's got to say, I will have something to say back. Never, ever go up against a smart woman. *We. Will. Crussssh. You.*

I circle my finger in the air, indicating that I have accepted his challenge to remain silent.

"Elle, these past few days, getting repeatedly rejected by you made me really stop and think. I mean, I've never tried so hard with a girl, and I had to ask myself why. Yes, I think you're my talisman. But why? Why would a girl who has been in my life for such a short period of time affect me so much? Sure. You're ridiculously smart and hot and you make me happy as hell when you let down your guard, which is really only about five percent of the time—not nearly enough. But when you do," he takes his fist and slams it over his heart, "it's like the fucking Fourth of July and a touchdown all rolled into one."

I'm suddenly thrown back a step by his corny words. He's trying to speak from his heart, and I can tell by his body language this is uncomfortable for him. It's kind of sweet.

Don't go all soft, Elle. This changes nothing, I say to myself as a reminder of why I should be pissed. He's making this unnecessarily painful. He needs to stop trying to back me into a corner.

I'm just going to have to play hardball and decapitate his ego so he accepts the truth and stops this nonsense for both our sakes.

He continues, "But, Elle, as hard as I tried, I couldn't figure it out. I don't know what you did to make me like you so much, but I realized I do. I like you a lot. And somehow, I can't move on from this," he points to the floor between us, "spot in my life until we have it out, so let me lay it all on the line for you." He draws a sharp breath and those green eyes are exploding with intensity. "You and me, we work. I don't know why. I don't even care why. But we do. So if you'd like to play your little games and pretend otherwise, be my guest." He points to himself. "*I* know the truth. And *I* see through you. The only thing I don't know is why you're throwing this giant wall between us, and that's why I'm here. My gut says you're afraid to go for it. And that's okay. I can wait. I can give you space to figure it all out. I can even just be your friend and hold your hand while you go through hell with your mother's situation. I am willing to be patient while you get to a place where you're ready for something serious. But what I can't tolerate," he shakes his big finger in my face, "is lies. So if you're really serious, Elle, and you really truly want nothing to do with me, then you just say so. But if you feel what I feel, that we could take on the fucking world together, then all I'm asking is for you to show up at the airport at eleven o'clock and come to Ohio with me tonight. Because I think I need you. And I think you need me too. And *that* is why I haven't been able to play football since we broke up."

My eyes tear up and, to my utter shock, I have absolutely nothing to say. Nothing. There's an avalanche of emotions crashing down inside me and they're bottlenecking at my mouth.

"I-I-I…" My mouth sort of just flaps while Henry's expression turns from serious to livid.

"Really? You're just going to stand there with your mouth shut?" he growls.

Yep. Looks that way. Because I'm paralyzed with fear. Nobody has ever said something that sounds so precariously close to a declaration of love, making me feel all vulnerable and wanted. But his statement simply doesn't make sense—I mean, why would anyone want me? I'm the girl who's never fit in. I'm not even a girl. I'm just a ball of middle-aged cynicism in the body of a nineteen-year-old.

He's…he's young and strong and so full of potential. He has his entire life to learn how hard things are out in the world.

I want to speak with brutal honesty, but I am unable to fully decipher my emotions—resentment that he's forcing me to feel things when I've reached my limit of feeling. Rage, because he has taken away the sliver of control I once had over my world. Sadness, because he's offering me something I want so badly. Frustration, because I don't know how to accept it. Regret, because I am simply not a stronger person.

He places his large hands on his waist and bobs his head towards his feet, blowing out a long whoosh of a breath. "Okay. Okay. Fine. I get it. But you're making a mistake, Elle. I'm not just a party guy. I don't just want to have fun. I'm ready for something more, and the proof is that yesterday I suddenly realized that something I used to think was everything doesn't really work without you."

Fuck. My heart cramps with angst.

Once again, I open my mouth, attempting to speak, but it doesn't happen. Not the way I want it to.

"I'm sorry," I mutter under a breath that threatens to become a sob.

"So am I, Elle. So am I."

He heads for the door and reaches for the handle. "Oh, I left a gift in your closet. I thought it might be a good way for us to start off on a new foot and learn how to be together, but feel free to return it. The receipt's in the box."

He leaves, slamming the door behind him. I stand there staring at the space he occupied a few moments before.

I feel like chasing after him, but I don't see the logic in "us" and I can't trust my emotions. After all, right now they're busy slobbering on themselves like a complete moron and poking their eyes with rubber forks.

"Elle?" Tassie's head of brown curls pops through the door. "Everything okay?"

I nod.

"I just saw Henry punching holes in the hallway. What happened?" she asks.

I shrug. "I'm not sure."

She walks over and takes my hand. "Well, what did he say?"

"I think he said he's in love with me, but not with those exact words."

"Really?" she practically squeals and covers her mouth. "So what did you say?"

"The only thing I could. Basically, no."

Her hands fall to her sides. "Really?"

I nod.

"And…how do you feel about that?" she asks.

"I feel like shit." I feel like I just made the wrong choice.

"*Meow! Meow.*"

"Errr…what's that?" Tassie asks.

I turn my head in the direction of the sound: the closet.

"*Meowww.*"

"Holy shit. Is that a cat?" Tassie goes over, and I watch as she slides out a cat carrier. Inside is a gray and white kitten.

"Ohmygod! Baby kitty, come here, you!" Tassie grabs the tiny thing and holds it to her chest. There's a card taped to the carrier, too, which Tass hands to me. "Think it's for you."

I take it and look inside.

It's time to move forward. With me. And Mr. Nucleus II.

Love,
Henry

"Well?" Tass asks. "What does the card say?"

That I've got to find a suitcase, wash clothes, buy cat food, and wax. "It says I just made a huge mistake. Can you cat sit tomorrow?"

Tassie smiles. "Love to."

CHAPTER NINE

HENRY

I know there is no point in playing today. My heart's not in the game and everyone knows it.

Man, she turned me down? I snap to myself. After I opened up and told her things I hadn't been ready to admit even to myself? And what kind of woman resists a guy who gives her a kitten? Because I'm sure she found it and she still didn't show up to the airport last night.

She must be some sort of supernatural being. A demon maybe. It's the only explanation for why I feel possessed by her.

I suit up and keep to myself. I've already decided to go out there and tell Coach I'll sit on the bench. There are a hundred scouts at this game, including the one who's made a preliminary offer to my agent. It was contingent upon my having a good season and not getting injured, of course. But I have to face facts—I never played the game in my head. I've always played with my heart. Maybe that's why I was better than most. But I never dreamed that a nerdy little chick with a genius IQ and a sharp tongue could work her way in and upset my mojo. Not after I'd already endured a hell of a lot of bullshit from my parents, who tried every emotional trick in the book to get me to stop playing football.

I'm the last to leave the locker room, following behind a small army of Pirates in their black and red uniforms. I walk straight over to the coach, who's talking to Hunter about a change in a play.

I wait for Coach to finish talking.

"What is it, Walton?" he snaps.

Hunter stares at me, and I see this weird look in his eyes. Like he's panicking or something.

That's kind of sweet, dude. But you guys will play better without me, I think to myself.

I look Coach squarely in the eyes. "I just wanted to tell you that I won't be—"

"Fucking up," Hunter interrupts. "He won't be fucking anything up because his new motivational coach is working out really well."

I look at Hunter, who mouths the word *Elle* and jerks his head over toward the stands.

Elle? Elle's here? I look for her smiling face but don't see it.

"Glad to hear it, Walton," Coach says. "But words don't impress me. I want solid defense today." He walks away, and I turn my attention back to Hunter.

"Tass texted me," he says. "Elle couldn't show up last night, so she needed to borrow money to buy a ticket for the first flight out this morning. I'm sure she's already here."

"Seriously?" I feel a rush in my veins and my heartbeat accelerates.

"Yeah, man." Hunter claps me hard on the back. "Now let's go kick some Ohio ass."

I can't believe it. My lucky charm decided to give me a chance. I don't know what makes me happier. That or the fact that I am going to kick ass while she watches and then spend the rest of the day and night kissing her, licking her, and fucking the hell out of her until she makes that little squeaky sound I love so much. It feels like my risk paid off, and now the pieces of my life are sliding back into place. With Elle by my side.

ELLE

I cannot believe how freaking awesome Henry is. It's like he's been pumped with Scooby snacks and is taking down everyone in his path like they were made of papier-mâché. I freaking hate football, but watching him break through the offensive line and sack the other team's quarterback ten times in one game is nothing shy of amazing. It's psychological warfare at its finest.

I think I might actually start liking this sport! I bet the data analysis part of it is fun.

Of course, what does data matter when the other side is so frustrated that they begin making random mistakes like dropping the ball and running into each other? I've never seen so many large men freaking the hell out, practically crying.

Damn. It's such a shame I couldn't be there, I think, watching on my tiny phone.

"Can't you go any faster? The game is almost over," I bark at the cab driver, who couldn't care less about my romantic predicament.

"This is the limit. I drive the limit. And it's not my fault you're late." He mumbles that last bit.

"It's not my fault either." I had a connecting flight in Denver and that flight got cancelled due to equipment issues. They put me on the first flight out, but then that flight got delayed due to weather. With any luck, I'll show up right as the stadium empties. But I need to be there. Henry needs to know I showed up—maybe not for the game, but for us.

Suddenly, I notice the cab's not moving. "What the hell?" I look up and there's a logjam.

"People must be leaving the game early—clogs up all the roads," says the driver.

"Early?" I feel my heart deflate. But of course they're leaving early. No one wants to stick around just to see their home team lose bigger.

I debate texting Henry and telling him I really tried to make it, but what good would it do? He's on the field. His cell is in the locker room.

Exhausted from flying all morning and being

stuck in airports, I fold my arms over my chest and close my eyes. Well, at least Henry's got his groove back. He played an awesome game. And now he and I can start off on a new foot. I guess today won't be a complete loss.

HENRY

I fucking crushed it today, and it's just one more piece of evidence that Elle and I belong together. I'm not saying I'm nothing without her, because I got where I am today on my own, but there's no doubt in my mind that she's the secret sauce moving forward.

The score? Sixty-two to seven.

"Great job, man." My teammates take turns patting my back. Of course, Hunter and our wide receiver, Ryan, scored all the touchdowns, but I shut out the other team's chance of scoring for over ninety percent of the game. It's the kind of moment sports-related wet dreams are made of.

We do the obligatory handshakes with the other team and I head over to the stands, which are already half empty. Any moment, I'm expecting to see Elle, with her little face and those giant glasses, to prance up and complete the victorious day.

But I wait and I wait. No Elle.

I look around the stadium and there's no sign of her. I see Hunter talking to a reporter, doing an interview. I don't do interviews because they always try to sneak in questions about my dad or the company.

"Hey, man, seen Elle?" I say to Hunter.

Hunter raises his finger to the woman holding a microphone. "Hold on. One second."

I repeat my question.

"Sorry. Can't say I have." Hunter goes back to his little moment in the spotlight and it dawns on me.

Elle's not here. Why would Hunter tell me she's here when clearly she's not?

"Wait. Did you lie?" I growl.

Hunter looks over at me. "No, man. I didn't lie. Tass said she was coming," he says dismissively.

I'm not buying it. I'm especially not buying the way Hunter is brushing me off. He fucking lied. I thought we were friends.

I grab his shoulder, spin him around, and then grab him by the jersey. "You fucking piece of shit."

"Get your hands off me, Henry," he growls.

"Or what?" I scowl back.

"What's the fucking deal? We won. You won. You didn't need her for that. It was all you, Henry. Be happy."

"So you did lie." I throw a punch, and it lands right on Hunter's jaw. He flies back with an *oomph!* and I seize the moment. I jump on top of him and cock my fist, but someone's grabbing my arm and people are yelling. In the recesses of my mind, I know it's my teammates. I know the cameras are rolling, too, but I don't care. My best friend fucking lied to me, after I helped him, gave him a place to live.

But maybe that's not really why I'm so mad. He just happens to be an easy outlet. Really, I'm pissed because Elle didn't come. Everything in my world felt right for a few short hours and then it was taken from me.

I manage to break free and tackle Hunter again, who's halfway up. I've got him pinned because I'm bigger and stronger than he is.

"You're right," I snarl. "I don't need her. And I don't need you. I never did." I land one more punch before I'm dragged off him. "You and her are just like my father, manipulative fucking liars. Tell Elle to go fuck herself. And you go with her."

From the corner of my eye I see two big brown eyes staring at me from behind chunky black glasses with the tape in the middle.

"Elle?" I pause my rant just long enough to watch her run the fuck away.

"Let me go!" I yell. "Elle! Elle!" She's gone before I have a chance to sort this shit out or come to grips with what I've just done. I've just fucked everything up. Everything. And I know that this time, there aren't enough kittens in the world to fix it.

ELLE

I can't believe what I just saw. This big beautiful man turned into a beast before my eyes, filled with rage and ready to tear apart his best friend in front of the world.

I don't believe for a moment that Henry is a violent man or would ever hurt me. That's not what this is about. The shocking part was that I saw myself in that moment; all the pain coming loose like an avalanche of emotions, unstoppable, crushing everything good in its path. It's exactly how I felt the moment I tore into Henry on Thanksgiving and told my father he was foolish for hoping.

That is what disturbs me; that I've just realized how similar Henry and I are. Yet you'd never, ever know it from simply looking at us. He's this huge guy, ripped from head to toe, awe-inspiring really. He has the kind of looks and confidence that open any door and draw people to him. Me? I'm five two and weigh a hundred and twenty pounds. I look like the girl who probably ate paste in the first grade, though I had really been making rockets. The kind you get national science fair awards for. But still, underneath it all, I've now realized that Henry and I are exactly the same—ready to tell the world to fuck off, filled with fight and a whole hell of a lot of resentment. It keeps us from trusting. It keeps us from connecting.

Still, it all starts making sense—why I was drawn to him and why I really didn't want to start a relationship. It was never about being different. It was always about the fear of having to take a good hard look at myself.

I start to laugh, snorting and hiccupping—the full nine yards. *Henry is me. Henry is me.* I can't control the goddamned need to laugh.

My phone beeps, and I slip it from my pocket, not even bothering to check the caller ID. I know it's Tass.

"He-hello?" I chuckle.

"Elle, honey, it's your dad."

"Dad?" My blood pressure takes a nosedive. "What's the matter?"

"Baby, it's your mother."

CHAPTER TEN

HENRY

Well, this isn't pretty, I think while watching a gif of myself punching Hunter, playing on *Sportsnet Today* while the hosts talk about the game.

Goddammit. National coverage has ensued, my emotional outburst seen by over twenty million people, likely including my parents. Now the rumors are flying that I'd been in a 'roid-rage. None of that really matters to the scouts, though, because now everyone thinks I'm some sort of tough guy who can take any team to victory. They're calling me the "Quarterback Crusher." Also, Hunter made a public statement apologizing for provoking the fight and for letting a little friendly "ball busting" get out of hand. He took a bullet for me—his way of saying he is sorry—but we both know it was all me. A giant man-tantrum over a girl.

I look over at Hunter, who is sitting at the kitchen table, studying for his English test, a huge shiner on his left eye.

"Man, I'm really sorry," I say.

Without lifting his eyes off his book, he replies with a shrug. "Dude, you have to stop apologizing every time you look at me."

"Can't help it," I mumble and turn my attention back to the TV.

"And turn that shit off," he says. "It's only making you feel worse."

I sigh and do it. The self-flagellation is probably pointless. I need to go see Elle and say I'm sorry. I just know it's better to have a cooling-off period after pissing someone off like I've done to her. I literally yelled to the entire world that I didn't need her.

"Think it's safe to go over to the dorms?" I ask.

"Elle's not there," Hunter mutters under his breath, highlighting something on the page. "She went home. Tassie went, too—wanted to bring Mr. Nibbles to cheer her up."

Huh? I turn my entire body in his direction. "It's Mr. Nucleus. And what happened? Is it Elle's mother?" I'm hoping it's not a turn for the worse.

Hunter lets out an exasperated sigh. "I don't know, Henry. Tassie doesn't want to talk about it right now—says she needs to focus on holding a rope or lifeline or some strange shit like that. And I'm not going to call Elle myself and pry."

"Why didn't you tell me?"

Hunter rolls his eyes. "Because whatever it is, I knew you'd just run over there and make a giant unwelcome ass out of yourself."

True. I would.

I scratch my beard. "But do you think it's bad?"

Hunter reaches for his pocket and produces his phone. "Dude, I don't know. Feel free to call Tass yourself, but I've learned my lesson with her. I don't butt in or come to the rescue unless she asks. She hasn't asked."

Pussy. I get up and go for his phone. It's already queued up to call Tass. I hear it ring twice before Tassie's voice comes on. "Hey, muffin nuts—sweet and delicious. Looking for some creamy butter?"

Ewww... And..."muffin nuts"?

I clear my throat. "I think my nuts are more like unripe kiwis. Firm, fuzzy, and not for eating. Licking is okay, though."

I hear Hunter chuckle.

"Who is this?" Tassie barks.

"Henry, who else?" I say.

"Ugh. What do you want, you big ogre? And why are you calling on Hunter's phone?"

"Because your boyfriend is a wuss and too afraid to ask you what's going on with Elle."

"Hold on," she says, followed by the sound of footsteps and a door closing. "What do you care, Mr. 'I don't need anyone'?" she hisses quietly. "And after all my hard work getting her to give you a chance."

"Tassie, I blew it. I know I did. But you know I care about Elle. I was just pissed. Tell me what's going on. Please."

I hear a long breath. "It's too depressing. I can't even say the words."

"Is she dying?"

"Yes, of course she is, you idiot."

I let that slide because I know that Tassie is under pressure.

She continues, "She started throwing up anything she ingests, so she's just not getting enough water or food. Her blood pressure is low, and she's unconscious half the time. They're debating what to do—hospitalize her, where she can be cared for by nurses, or leave her at home. No one can decide because Elle's mom told everyone she didn't want to go back to any depressing hospitals ever again, but they don't exactly know how to take care of her here. It's beyond devastating."

It's not like me to say something so sentimental and all touchy-feely, but, "Thank you for being there for Elle, Tassie. You're a good friend."

It makes me feel better knowing she's got someone close to her right there, even though I want that person to be me.

"Yeah, well," she says, "I'm sure Elle would do the same for any of us. And since I don't have money, I can't help out with the medical costs. This is all I can give."

Her comment gives me an idea. My only question is, what will my father ask for in return? He always wants something—like a piece of my soul—and since I basically called him a manipulative asshole on live TV, I'm fairly sure the price tag on any assistance just went through the roof.

I'll call my oldest sister. She runs all of the family's charities and sits on the board of a major hospital in Houston. She can help. Though she's just like my dad and will want something in return, it will be preferable to my father's demand.

"I'll call you back," I say.

"Why?" Tassie questions.

"I know a few people who can help—with nurses and stuff."

"Henry," she says sternly, "a nurse is nice, but her mother needs an act of god. So unless you know someone on the board of Paloverde Pharmaceuticals or you have a direct line to an angel, the best thing you can do is leave Elle alone."

I feel my gut twist into a painful knot. I know that company. All too well. "Paloverde Pharmaceuticals? Why them?"

"They're this company my mother and I have been hounding for days. They just released some new drug that might help, but we can't get anyone there to talk to us about helping Elle's mom."

I swallow a lump in my throat, but it does little to quell the acid spike in my stomach. My family's company acquired a majority share of Paloverde last month as part of their portfolio diversification. I know this because I'll be interning there next summer as part of my payment for the apartment and as part of my dad's master plan to teach me managerial skills.

Fuck. Fuck. Fuck. I want to hit something. I want to break, tear, scream, and roar. However, all I can manage is a nod and a, "Yup. Consider it done."

"Consider what done?" Tassie snaps.

"What's the name of the drug, Tassie?" I snarl.

"Henry, do *not* fuck with me."

"I wouldn't dare," I reply.

"So you know someone there?"

"Yes."

A long pause precedes a longer sigh. "Jesus, Henry. I swear to fucking God..." Her voice trails off.

"What?"

"Nothing." I know she wants to threaten death if I don't deliver. "I'll text you the information on what she needs—but please, please don't tell Elle anything unless you are one hundred and ten percent sure you can get this drug. She'll be—"

"Devastated." Which is exactly how I feel in this moment.

Wearing the obligatory suit and tie, I take the elevator to the top floor of Walton, Inc. As many times as I've been here, I've never gotten used to it. Stale air. Stale people. It feels like the life has been sucked out of everything here.

I walk up to Megan, my father's assistant, who's

in her late fifties but looks like she's a decade older—my father's fault, no doubt.

"Good morning, Megan." I offer her my most charming smile.

"Henry, so nice to see you. I actually have some paperwork for you to sign. Your father is making you majority shareholder of Johnson and Sons, a new bamboo-farming acquisition."

I grumble disapprovingly. My dad likes to put our names on things for tax purposes, but he runs everything. I generally go with it, just as long as he leaves me alone about football. Of course, that'll now be over.

"I'll sign on the way out. He's in today, right?" I ask.

"He's on call until eleven. Then, well…you know." She winks.

My dad takes a break every day at eleven in the morning. He gets naked—completely—lays out his yoga mat, and then gets into a pose and holds it for thirty minutes. It's weird as shit, but he claims that it focuses his mind and connects him to the power of his masculine energy or some bullshit like that. Seriously, the only thing that man is connected to is his wallet. Sadly, this is the only time of day I know he won't be on a call or in a meeting.

"I just need a minute. Thanks, Meg." I walk past her and go inside. My father is on his headset, facing his floor-to-ceiling window overlooking downtown Houston. There is only one picture of us—one of those horrible professional family portraits that's framed and mounted to the wall. Everything else in his office is sterile—glass coffee table, gray sofa with gray rug, black chairs, black desk, and not much else. The lack of life mirrors the rest of this company. Is there really any wonder I don't want to work here?

Yet you know exactly how this conversation is going to go…

My father notices me standing there and jerks his head, giving me the one-minute finger sign.

I take a seat in the leather chair facing his desk. I need to be firm. I need to be calm. I need his help, but I can't let this cost me everything. Still, my chances of leaving here unscathed are—

"So how much?" my father barks.

I look up at him, unsure if he's talking to me.

"Sorry?"

My father takes off his headset and leaves it on his desk. He's a big man, like me, but with a small beer belly and a blond crew cut.

"Henry, you only come to my office when you need money. Of course, you already have a trust fund and monthly allowance, so I'm guessing you're in trouble. Or you got someone else in trouble. Who is she?"

I shake my head. This conversation has already started off on a sour note—his only note—but I have to do this. For Elle.

"I don't need money. I need your help. There's

a friend of mine—yes, a girl—but her mother is—"

"I'm not a charity, Henry. And if you need help with some fundraiser, talk to your sister Claire. Now, if you'll excuse me, I have work to do. Not all of us get to spend our days dicking around with balls."

Ah, the obligatory football jab. It doesn't affect me. Not anymore. "Trust me, if Claire could help, I wouldn't be here. I need to—"

An alarm goes off on my dad's desk, and I know what it means. Yoga time. Now *that* definitely affects me.

"Eleven o'clock!" My father claps his hands and then starts loosening his tie.

Oh hell. I better speak fast, or I'll have to talk to his bare, hairy ass sticking up in the air. There are no words.

"Dad, I'm not going to bullshit you. That pharmaceutical company you just bought has a new drug—for treating tumors. I need it. For a friend's mother who's really sick."

My dad gets to work on the buttons of his shirt. "No problem."

No problem? That doesn't sound like him.

"Just tell her to pay one hundred thousand dollars like everyone else," he adds.

Ah, there's the greedy father I know. "Dad, come on. She can't afford that, and we can."

My father lays his shirt and tie over the back of his chair, giving me a nice view of his flabby pecs.

"Henry, I bought that company because of that drug and the money it will make. I can't just go giving it all away."

"I'm not asking for all, I'm asking for one patient."

"We have a study group. Tell her to apply like everyone else."

"She doesn't have time. We help her, or she dies," I say.

My father unzips his black slacks and slides them down, leaving him in his tightie whities.

Oh, geesh. I better close the deal quickly or I'm going to be looking at his frank and beans. And, for the record, I don't think I can win any conversation with my father while he's just standing there buck naked. Seriously disturbs me.

"I'm sorry to hear that, Henry. But you need to become accustomed to the idea that when you're a Walton, everyone wants handouts. If we said yes, then we'd have nothing left. That's not to say we're uncharitable—we raise millions every year—but we give it away in ways that help us maximize the tax write-offs."

The underwear comes off, and I have to fight my gag reflex. *Jesus, this man has no shame.*

I squirm in my chair and attempt to avert my eyes. "It's one person," I argue. "One person I care about."

Naked as a baby, all his junk just hanging there, he slides out a purple yoga mat from his desk drawer. *Please don't bend over, please don't bend over.*

"Sorry, Henry, the answer is no. I pay for your school, apartment, car, expenses and everything else. You want more, you'll have to work for it."

"You mean work for *you.*"

He gives me a look and spreads out his mat like he's about to do something casual like look at a map. He gets down on his hands and knees; thankfully, his ass is facing away. Still, the view is unnerving. "Feel free to work for someone else, but I doubt anyone is going to pay you as much, and you know how I feel about family loyalty."

The catch is that on my own, I could make really great money playing football, but I'm not pro yet. I still need to graduate and negotiate a contract with one of these teams. Even if I get a signing bonus, all this will take time. Weeks at best, months at worst. Elle's mother doesn't have that long.

"How about a loan?" I offer. "I'll pay you back as soon as I sign with a team."

My father shuts his eyes and lets out a slow meditative breath. "You have no collateral."

"I'm your son."

"Which is why your place is here with me," he says in a pseudo-calm tone and then ass goes in the air. His big hairy ass.

Gah! No. Why? "You know I love football. It's the only thing I want to do. If I come here, I'll hate it." *And I'll hate you.*

"Life isn't easy, Henry," he grunts toward the

floor. "It requires making tough choices and sacrifices, something you don't know anything about because we've given you everything. It's time you grow up and learn how the real world operates."

He's asking me to choose between playing in the NFL, something I've dreamed of since I could hold a football, and saving Elle's mother. I can't think of anything more fucked up.

Still, I've lost this conversation, and I can't reason with a disgusting hairy ass. I get up and head for the door. "The only problem, Dad, is that your world is all about money, greed, and control. Nothing thrives in it."

"Don't like the way things are? Then learn the ropes and change it. It'll all belong to you and your sisters someday."

"They can have it," I say, closing the door behind me.

"Ready to sign?" Meg asks, sliding a folder toward me across the desk.

I stare at her for a moment, not seeing her or anything around me. All I hear are my dad's brutally honest words. He's right. I've never had to make a sacrifice for anything. Not for my family, not for my education, and certainly not for any of my friends. Whenever I need something, it's always there. As for Elle, we've only known each other for a short time, but I know I couldn't ever face her or get on that field again, knowing it cost Elle's mother her life. I'm not a monster like my father.

"Henry?" Meg says.

"Tell my father he won. I'll come on board full-time starting in May." I take a piece of paper from a notepad on her desk, grab a pen, and jot down Elle's address and phone number. "This is the information of the woman I just told my father about." I hand the piece of paper to Meg. "Tell my dad to make sure she gets the medicine and treatment starting today or the deal's off. And make it anonymous."

Meg nods slowly, noting the devastation on my face. "Of course."

"Thanks."

"You'll do good things here, Henry. I know you will."

I nod, wondering what she really means by that. Maybe she refers to the lifeless atmosphere or ruthless corporate culture my father's created. I know he pays well, but that doesn't mean people are happy.

Well, guess I'll get to find out. Next spring, I'll be helping run the Walton empire. My only hope is to find a way to keep Elle in my life.

CHAPTER ELEVEN
ELLE

It's been one hell of a week. A bona fide plethora of sticky emotions that started out in the worst possible, darkest place, and then turned itself around in the matter of a day. I owe it all to Tassie's mother, who somehow managed to get my mother into a private, anonymously funded room in Houston's Mercy Hospital. They have one of the best oncology departments in the country.

The most amazing part, however, is that the doctors at the hospital and Tassie's mother pulled off a miracle. We got it. The medicine. Literally, I cried for an hour when I heard the news. But nothing topped the look on my father's face when I told him. He hugged me so hard that my ribs are sore. "I love you, little Elle. I love you so much," he'd said, nearly sobbing, making me cry right along with him.

But I won't lie. There was a moment when my brain urged me to temper his excitement with facts. This drug isn't a cure. It's a treatment. And treatments don't always work. So I quickly reminded myself that we all needed to focus on a positive outcome if we wanted to give my mom a fighting chance.

Anyway, she started the new drug almost immediately. Not a trial patient, not a placebo, but the real thing. And it's been shown to turbo-charge the immune system so that the body fights off the cancer on its own. In short, this is her best shot at making it, and I am committed to being hopeful. Besides, miracles like these just don't fall out of the sky for no reason.

"Hey, I'm going to get something greasy for lunch and run home to feed Mr. Nucleus," I whisper to my dad, who's sitting in the chair beside my mother's hospital bed, reading a book. With the care she's been getting, her vitals have improved, but she's still sleeping a lot. "Can I bring you anything back?"

"No, thanks, baby," he says.

"You sure?" I got here around ten in the morning, and he hasn't moved or eaten.

"If I get hungry, I'll run downstairs." He flashes a warm smile that shows in his brown eyes, which I love seeing.

"Okay. When she wakes up, tell Mom that I'll be back later."

"Take your time. Get some fresh air," he says.

I know I look like I could use it. Hospitals are not my favorite place. Especially since my mother's been in and out of them for almost two years.

I take the elevator down and head outside to the back parking lot. The afternoon air is crisp and cool, and I already feel lighter.

"Elle, hey," I hear a deep familiar voice say.

"Henry?" My mind snaps to attention and I spot him walking toward me in his jeans and plain blue Polo shirt. His green eyes look a little tired, but he is as beautiful as ever and my heart does this crazy little pitter-patter. "How'd you know where I was?"

"I went by your dorm room a few times this week, but you weren't there. Then I saw Tassie this morning, and she told me the good news."

"Oh. Yeah, I've been here all week."

He bobs his head. "I heard. You got a minute?"

I've been meaning to call him, actually. After Ohio and his big public episode with Hunter, I've wanted to tell him so many things. Mostly, that I'm not mad about what he said. I get why he was angry. But the moment I understood how similar he and I are, with our crazy walls and apprehension to trust, I realized the problem was never him. It was painful to admit, but it was always me. After feeling alone for so long, I just don't know how to share my life with a man. Especially one that forces me to take a good hard look at myself—walls, battle scars, self-perpetuated lies, and all.

The only solution I can think of is to take it slow. Friendship first. Only, I know it's not what he wants, and standing here looking at him now, the hunger in his vivid green eyes and slight tension in his angular jaw, friendship isn't what I want either. I want to rewind the clock and go back to that moment in my dorm room last Friday and say what I now know I feel: "*I think you might be right. I might need you, too.*" But I didn't say it. And now, I'm not sure how. Fact is, I'm just not as brave as he is. Fact is, I care about him and have to wonder if he's ready for my world. It's not exactly an easy place.

Let him decide, Elle. He laid his heart out there. Now, it's your turn.

"Elle? I promise this will only take a minute," he says.

Nope. This conversation is going to take much longer. But I need time to warm up. I hadn't planned on doing this today.

"Actually," I say, "I was just thinking of getting something to eat. They only have salads and healthy crap here. I need a bacon cheeseburger or something fattening. Wanna join me?"

I can't read his expression, exactly. But he's not smiling, not his usual self.

"I already ate," he says, "but I know a place that makes a respectable grilled cheese. I'll drive. My car's right over there."

I notice he's parked in a reserved space. Such a cocky guy. Thinks he can park anywhere. Of course, I like that about Henry. He acts like the world is his oyster. That's because it is.

"Thanks." I head for his SUV, my hands as tight as my stomach.

He unlocks the doors and opens the passenger side for me. I slip into my seat, unable to stop checking him out. Something's off. Something's really off. Like he's aged ten years despite looking like his same, youthful, stunningly handsome self.

Damn, I just can't put my finger on it. Maybe it's because he's not smiling. Maybe he's nervous because he thinks I'm going to tear into him.

Best let him off the hook. I'll need his full attention for what I have to say.

He starts the engine and pulls out into the parking lot, immediately heading toward downtown.

"Henry." I clear my throat. "I want you to know that I'm not mad about what you said in Ohio. So there's no need to apologize. In fact—"

"You're not mad?"

"No," I say. "I know you were just upset when I saw you at the game."

"Then why are you still blocking my number?"

I am? "With all the commotion around my mom, I guess I just forgot."

Henry takes a right turn. I guess he knows where he's going, because he doesn't use maps or anything. I hardly ever come into Houston except for the rare shopping trip or to go to the airport— too much traffic.

I'm about to begin the painful process of open

honesty, when he cuts in.

"So," he says, keeping his intense eyes on the road, "now that your mom is being taken care of, I'm sure it's a huge relief."

"Oh. Yeah. I mean, we're not even close to being out of the woods, but at least we have hope now. And she's a fighter. If anyone can make it through this, she can. Especially now that she's starting this new treatment. Statistically, her chances are sixty percent."

"Is that good?"

"It was zero last weekend, so I'd say yes. Plus, Tassie's mother has been giving me information on all of the other things we can do to help, like diet and meditation. There's a special kind of yoga she can try—I hear it helps the body heal."

Henry grumbles something about yoga under his breath. Guess he's not a fan.

"So when are you coming back to school?" he asks.

"I'm not. I've decided to drop out, which leads me to—"

"What?" He glances at me for a moment but quickly returns his eyes to the road. "You're dropping out?"

"My family needs me," I explain, "and I've had to face some hard truths lately."

"But school, Elle. You're so smart. Why wouldn't you want a degree?"

It's not who I am. "I thought it was the right

thing to do, but now I know it was a mistake."

Henry is silent on the matter, but I can tell from his flexing jaw muscles and the eagle-like intensity in his eyes, he's bothered.

"What?" I say.

"Nothing. So you're really not coming back?"

I debate my next words carefully because the pretend Elle would make up some bullcrap and say something a normal person might about how college is so important. It is, but I'm not normal. So I opt for being honest with Henry and taking a baby step toward telling him who I really am.

"I never wanted to go to college," I confess. "Besides, I've already read the books in all my classes. Ten years ago. And now I'm realizing that it's a waste of time going through the motions of getting a degree just to make someone else happy."

"Make who happy?" Henry flashes me a confused look.

"My mom. She's the one who wanted me to go to school. I think it's just the way she was raised. You go to college, get a job, get married, have kids and then you retire. That's not me."

"So no marriage and kids for you, huh?"

"Why, you asking, Henry?" I joke, but he doesn't laugh with me.

"You never know." He pulls up to a stoplight and looks at me. "Elle, are we back on, or are we over?"

Suddenly, my heart starts going all crazy and my

toes are tingling. "Well—" I swallow whatever's in my throat, probably my ability to keep a clear head. "I think I want to crawl before I walk. And you and I are in different preschools. We're crawling in different directions."

"I thought you showed up to the game in Ohio because you wanted to give us a shot?" he says.

"I did. I do. But you have to understand, Henry. I'm conflicted over us. I was forced to grow up so fast, and I don't want that kind of accelerated life for you. I want you to savor every minute and enjoy it. And I definitely don't want to be the person who gets in the way of your dream. It just wouldn't be right."

"That's not your choice," he scowls.

Oh no. The conversation is going sideways. *Regroup. Regroup.*

"Henry, let's be honest. I can't see how I can do all the things I want in life and be with you, a guy who travels all the time, going to games, having women throw themselves at him."

Wait. That came out wrong. I'd merely wanted to point out how our lives are in different places and I'm not sure what to do about it.

His sensual lips flatten and his large hands tighten around the steering wheel. "So you've already dismissed us? Completely."

"No! I haven't. But I need someone who will be there to build a life with me, Henry. You're still a big kid—just as you should be."

Ugh! Foot in mouth! Why, why do I suck at this so badly!

"You're wrong about me, Elle." The light turns green, and instead of continuing down the street, he takes a left into an underground garage. Above it is a huge high-rise building.

"Where are we going?" I ask.

"The best place for grilled cheese in Houston."

It doesn't look like the sort of building that has a restaurant, but okay. I'm too busy trying to pry my mouth out of my ass. My next words need to be clear and precise. *Thinking, thinking, thinking...*

We pull up to a set of elevators and a valet shows up, opening the door for me. I get out and Henry hands the guy the keys.

Still thinking, thinking, thinking...Ugh! I don't know what to say and how to make it come out the right way.

Once inside, Henry scans a card and the elevator doors pop open. It's a regular elevator with numbers on the buttons. Usually, when there are businesses in a place like this, the name of the company is somewhere close to the buttons.

"This is a residential building, isn't it?" I ask.

Facing the doors, he nods. "Yep."

"So why have you brought me here?"

"Because we're going to my apartment, and I'm making you lunch."

Huh? I know Henry's family is wealthy, but Henry has an apartment off campus back in Austin.

He never mentioned another place.

"So this is what, your weekend bachelor pad?" *Still thinking, thinking and…nothing!* "Henry, let's be friends, because I really want to sleep with you." *No. No. That's weird.* "Henry, I am a giant antisocial crazy person, but let's take it slow." *Ugh. Worse!* "Henry, I am afraid. I'm so, so afraid because you're so, so wonderful. And if it didn't work out, it might really, really hurt." *No! Too needy.*

"Bachelor pad?" Henry huffs. "Not exactly."

The elevator opens on the top floor and my mouth drops. It's got a panoramic view of Houston.

"Wow. This is…this is…impressive," I say.

"It's a perk of my new job. A penthouse in the city. A weekend house wherever I want."

I blink at him. "What job?"

"Helping my father run his company after college."

Whoa. Whoa. Whoa. Stop the presses. What's going on here? Because while I've been agonizing over my big emotional premier party, I've clearly missed something.

"How are you going to have time for football?" I ask.

"I won't. I'm giving it up."

Whatthefuck?

"That doesn't make any sense," I protest. "I mean, you love football. And I don't just mean like. You loooove it." Plus, Hunter told me that Henry's dad is a huge greedy asshole.

"Everyone's gotta grow up sometime. Don't they, Elle?" He gestures over to the kitchen area, which is a big open space on the other side of the living room area. It's got stainless steel everything, glass cabinets and marble counters.

I'm shocked. Really shocked. Usually, I'm great at figuring things out—like in those crazy spy novels I love so much, but something's not computing.

"Henry, was this really your choice?"

"Yes."

"Did your dad pressure you?" I ask.

"Since I was born."

"Okay, but did something new happen? Something that made you change your mind about the sport you love more than life itself?"

"I already told you, you were wrong about me. Football isn't everything." Henry pulls out an apron from a drawer after checking three or four of them. Clearly, he doesn't know his way around this kitchen, but he knows how to make a grilled cheese because he's got out a pan, butter, cheese and bread. I'm guessing that grocery shopping comes with the package because this penthouse looks expensive, and I can't see Henry doing the whole supermarket thing.

"I guess…I don't know what to say." I watch him drop a pat of butter into the warm pan. I can't help focusing on how he seems so different. More grown up maybe? And he's ditching football of his own accord, which means our relationship's probability of success just became a positive integer. A really, really big positive integer. *Why doesn't that make me happy?* It's like I've just gotten everything I wanted, but everything feels off, tainted and airless.

"Is it stuffy in here?" I ask.

"I feel okay, but the thermostat is right over there by the front door."

I definitely need cooler air. I hop up and go fiddle with the thing, setting the temperature to seventy-two. From the corner of my eye, I see his bedroom. It's got a huge bed and hardwood floors. From the light pouring in, I know there are more views and big windows. Maybe one of them opens and I can hang my head out of it.

I walk over to investigate while my brain is crunching on all this.

"Wow," I whisper, pushing the door wide open. It's like something straight out of an interior design magazine. Alternating light gray and white walls. Highly polished hardwood floors. Sleek modern furniture—red and white. There's a private patio with a gas fire pit and a hot tub, all overlooking the city.

I slide the door open and a slight breeze washes over my face. I inhale deeply, trying to settle my thoughts. Part of me is selfishly happy about Henry's decision because it means we might have a future. On the other hand, it's not making sense that he'd quit. Really, it's not. Something happened.

"Like the view?" says Henry, startling me from

behind.

I jolt and turn, placing my hand over my heart. "Oh. You scared me."

"Sorry. Your sandwich is ready." He's still wearing his black apron, and I can't help notice how it barely covers his broad chest, a chest I really, really miss touching.

"So fast?"

"You've been gone for five minutes. I thought maybe you'd gotten distracted by the big bathroom."

"Oh. No. I haven't gotten past your patio. It's spectacular."

He makes a little shrug. "Yeah. I guess it's nice. But the place feels more like a hotel than a home."

"You're really going to live here?"

"I own it now, so I guess I should."

I narrow my eyes. "But you never mentioned wanting this or quitting football or—"

"Elle, we've both admitted that there's still a lot we don't know about each other."

"But something is not—"

Henry suddenly bends down and kisses me. His lips are warm and soft. The scruff around his mouth is bristly and rough. The moment his hot tongue slides through my lips and I taste him on my tongue, I realize that I've missed this. I've missed the way he smells—sweet, clean, manly, and a tinge of bad boy.

He pulls back, and I stare up at him, noticing

how serious he seems now. Or maybe he was more mature than I'd given him credit for. I chose to see what I wanted.

Slowly, he takes his hand and pushes a lock of my hair behind my ear. "I've missed you, Elle."

"I've missed you, too," I say, my body unable to get enough air. He's standing too close.

"I'm glad we finally agree on something." He leans down and kisses me again. His strong arms snake around my waist, pulling me into the heat of his large frame. An intoxicating rush of excitement floods my body. This is what I like about being with Henry. He knows just how to use every inch of himself—the right way to hold me, the way to make me feel like I belong to him.

I throw myself into the kiss, cupping his rough cheeks with my hands.

He lifts me effortlessly and carries me over to the bed. My mind forgets all the worries and squabbles of the past few months. I can't even remember why I wanted to stop seeing him. Because Tassie was right, we do have chemistry. I'm reminded of it every time I look into his eyes and feel something beyond just physical attraction.

Henry pulls his shirt over his head, and I drink in the masculine vision of perfection before me—his ripped abs and dusting of light brown hair on his lower stomach; the swell of his biceps and his broad shoulders. I love how despite his magnificent size, our bodies always fit together perfectly.

Those green eyes are intense and locked on my face as he unbuttons the top of his jeans, revealing a patch of dark hair and his long, thick cock. I lick my lips and open my legs for him.

I'm still dressed. Why am I still dressed? I kick off my low tops and unbutton my jeans. Henry watches as I wiggle my way out of my pants.

"Gonna take off that top?" He grins.

"Oh. Yeah. I almost forgot." I didn't, of course. I am just feeling greedy and anxious to get that hard cock inside me.

I grab the hem of my T-shirt and pull it over my head. The bra follows quickly and Henry just stands there staring at me with this look in his eyes.

"What's wrong?" I ask.

"Nothing."

I don't believe him, but clearly he's not ready to open up. Like me, he just needs time. *Maybe I'll juggle for him later.* It'll be a nice icebreaker. Intro to Elle 101.

"Well," I say, with a sigh, thinking aloud, "I guess now that you're giving up football, we'll have a lot more time to get to know each other." I like that idea. I'm just not sure I like how it came about.

Henry's nostrils flare a little, and I can see his chest rising and falling. I can't tell if he's turned on or a little irritated or both.

He leans forward and joins me on the bed, capturing my mouth with an aggressive kiss, like he's got something to say and wants to show me with his body. His tongue is demanding, his grip on the back of my neck is firm, and his body is tense. He pushes me back and stares hungrily at me for a moment before reaching for my waist and flipping me over. With his size and strength, he has no problem maneuvering my petite body.

I hear him grab for something in the nightstand and see him toss a condom wrapper to the floor. I'm glad he remembered because I'm too caught up in him and us to think of anything else.

He grips my hips, forcing me onto my elbows. With one quick thrust, he takes me from behind, sliding deep. My breath whooshes from my lungs, and I wince. I had not been expecting that. He always plays with me first. He loves to mess around and goof off and make me laugh a million times with raspberries on my thigh or licking me in that ticklish spot behind my knee. He definitely likes foreplay, too. He's great at it.

Henry pulls out and slams into me again, driving deep. I'm shocked by the fierceness of his thrusts and the hard way he's fucking me. There's anger in it. There's despair in it. I'm not afraid, it's not like that. I feel more confused than anything.

Henry begins pumping hard with his hips, driving in and pulling out at a ferocious pace. I brace my arm on the headboard, thinking that whatever this is, he sure as hell isn't thinking about my needs because there is no way I'll come like this, and he knows it. Nor does he seem to care.

No juggling for you!

Henry hammers into me, his large hands holding my hips so he can angle the head of his thick cock deeper. It's to a point where I can't take more of him, but he drives again and then stills with a deep guttural groan, coming inside me. I feel his cock twitching out his cum, which makes me feel fifty degrees hotter. Now my c-spot is throbbing, wanting more. My nipples ache for the hard suction of his mouth.

Henry pulls out and lets go. I expect him to slap my ass or something—he always loves to hear me yelp a little. But that's that. He's gone into the bathroom, leaving me on all fours with my ass in the air.

Jesus, what just happened?

I get dressed and then go to the guest bathroom near the entryway to clean up. When I come out, Henry's in the kitchen, putting the frying pan in the sink, and putting away the butter and cheese.

"Henry?" I say quietly. "What was that?"

He doesn't look at me.

"Henry?"

"Let me take you home," he grumbles.

"Eh…no. You just rode me like a pony strapped with dynamite."

He gives me a hard look and goes back to cleaning up.

"That was a joke, Henry. Get it…if he's got dynamite, you won't want to stay on him too long."

"Are you going to eat?"

Okay. I'm missing something. Perhaps my over-joyed state due to my mother's improved outlook has clouded my ability to see the pieces.

All right. Deep breath. Think.

Henry is quitting football and leaving behind his dreams for the NFL. He's going to work for his wealthy a-hole of a father. Henry doesn't seem like the material-istic type in that he doesn't wear expensive clothes, never brags about anything but his awesome "game," and never discusses how freakishly wealthy his family is. Yet here he is in a penthouse. Angry. In a penthouse he wanted to show me. Why?

My brain throws out a few horrible answers, but the only one that makes sense is… "Please don't call me a pompous bitch for saying this, but, Henry, did you give up football for me?" I mean, I did tell him—at least twice—that he wasn't a serious person and that I needed a man. A grown-up man.

He looks at me. "What makes you think that?"

"Uh-uh. Don't play games, Henry. If you want us to have a shot, then this is the point you step up and answer honestly." I run my hands through my hair, praying he did not just alter the course of his lifelong trajectory for my sake.

"Yes."

My mouth drops. "No. No. No. Why? Why would you do that? I never meant for you to give up everything just to please me. I meant that we were different and on different paths and that was reality.

I never intended for you to go out and try to be someone you're not. That's ridiculous."

"You did it for your mother. You just told me so."

I'm about to protest, but he's got me on that. "Yes. I did go to college to make my mom happy. But I also told you that I'm correcting the situation. Henry, if being with you means that you have to give up who you are, then I don't want it. Not like this. Not at this price."

No wonder he passive-aggressive humped me.

"Well," he says, "I didn't quit football to please you. And what's done is done. I can't go back."

"Of course you can. You just walk up to your coach and say I want to play. Boom. You're back." No team lets go of a player like Henry voluntarily. And yes, I've been stalking him on social media and in the sports news. I know his career just grew rocket boosters. He's the talk of the town, the belle of the beefcake ball.

"No, Elle. I really can't. I've made a commitment. I have one semester left after finals and then I'm SVP of Walton, Inc., and CEO of several subsidiaries."

"Oil. You're going to work for big oil." I roll my eyes. If he thinks this will win me over, he's got another think coming.

"Not all oil. My father's been investing in other ventures. He knows oil isn't the future, but he needs help and I can't complain about the money."

Whoa. Henry's never cared about money. Not in the greedy, sell-your-soul sort of way. His father must've made some sort of threat or had some new leverage…

This is the part where my brain does stuff I don't ask it to. It's almost like having neuropathways made up entirely of bullet trains that travel at the speed of light.

The lightbulb flickers, and I tilt my head. That's it. Henry paid for my mother's care. Or he had a hand in it. I mean, angels just don't fall out of the sky and give people medicine in a day and the best doctors money can buy. Henry had once mentioned his father didn't approve of the whole football thing and that Henry always had to pay with his time.

I cover my mouth and my eyes tear up. "Oh, Henry," I gasp. "You didn't. You didn't. Please tell me you didn't."

He looks at me, and I see it in his eyes.

"Oh, Henry," the tears begin to stream down my cheeks, "you did. You asked him for help, and he made you give up football, didn't he?"

Henry lets out a slow breath toward the floor.

"Goddammit. No." I sigh. "Why didn't you tell me?"

"And say what? That my father is a supreme heartless asshole who owns the drug company making your mother's medicine and that he told me to choose between helping her or something he knows I love."

I cup my hands over my face. "Oh, God," I whisper. It's worse than I thought. I'd assumed Henry had asked for a loan or something. But his father owns the company and used it to blackmail Henry?

This man has got to be the world's biggest prick. "No wonder you didn't want to work for him."

Henry scratches the back of his neck. "It doesn't matter now. I've agreed. He's making sure your mom is getting what she needs, and I'm not about to risk that just because I love to throw balls around on a grass field with a bunch of big dudes."

I walk around the counter and throw my arms around his neck, pushing up on my tiptoes. I was so, so wrong about what I'd been thinking earlier. This version of him isn't mature. It's the sad version. He's heartbroken. That's where all of the seriousness came from. That's why he seems so different.

"I changed my mind. I like the guy who wants to play and have fun and work hard for what he wants, because that's the guy who just gave it all up. For me." I push my mouth to his and pour my gratitude and my "I'm so, so sorries" into the kiss. I drink him in and let go for the first time in my life. I really don't give a lab rat's ass if he wants to make football his life because I know how to make things work, and I know a man like him is so hard to find.

He holds me by the waist and returns my kiss,

but then pulls away.

Those green eyes pierce me, and I can hardly breathe just standing here looking at him.

He whisks away a tear trickling down my chin. "Please don't cry. I am going to survive. I promise there are worse fates."

"I know, but you deserve better. You deserve to live your dream, Henry." And I'm not about to let him give it up.

"Aside from the obvious parental shortcomings, I've always had everything I've wanted." He draws a smooth breath. "But now I found something I *need*, and if I'm lucky, I'll get to deserve her."

Gahhh...Heart expanding. Must. Relieve. Pressure. Must open it. "Marry me!"

Henry jerks back his head and blinks at me. "Sorry?"

"Marry me."

"Errr...you feeling okay, Elle?"

"Yes. Very okay. My brain did the computation, and you are my ideal match. Out of seven point five billion people on the planet, there is no one who has ever made me feel like this, and the probability of finding a man who is more handsome, fit, or intelligent than you, who also has an abundantly sized penis and healthy-sized ego—but not completely overbearing—who genuinely cares about me and will give me really strong swimmers when I'm ready; and who will also be able to lift me when I'm eighty because I have a fifty-two-point-seven chance of falling and breaking a hip; and who will also likely still be alive when I'm eighty because he exercises more than one hour a day; and—"

"Elle, enough already."

"*And…*" I hold up a finger, "who will do anything to make sure I'm okay." I poke his chest. "You are literally one in seven point five billion, Henry. I can't afford to let you go," I say, staring into his eyes, trying to make him see that I'm anything but joking. "Oh, and I was once a clown and traveled with the circus. But that was a long time ago. Totally over."

"Huh?"

"Never mind. I love you. Will you please put aside the fact that we've only known each other for a short period of time, most of it having wild fantastic sex, and that I'm a woman—therefore breaking the proposal rules—and agree to be my husband? We don't need to marry today—we're young. But I need you to know I'm committed." I take his hand and hold it up to my mouth. "Please, Henry, if there's any doubt in your mind, then trust your heart. And if that still doesn't get you there, then trust *me*." I draw a quick breath. "Because I'm really fucking smart. Which is why I listened to *you*. We do work."

He blinks for ten long seconds, and I can see his wheels turning. He has to realize that *he* was the one who saw it first. *He* told me we worked. I just hadn't been ready to see it.

A slow, seductive smile creeps across his face. "Would you object to getting married at a football game? I always thought that looked cool."

I'm not sure if he's joking, but I don't really care. "So you're talking tailgate party instead of a reception?"

"That's a great idea." He laughs and kisses me. I feel this warm vibe encircle my entire body, and my mind—without my asking—tells me that this is what happens when people find true love. Their entire beings vibrate on the same frequency. They sync up. They go from being two separate organisms floating in the sea of life, to being two united forms rowing in one boat.

I break our kiss. "You really want a football wedding?"

"You were really in the circus?"

I tilt my head and shrug. "Yeah."

"That's so hot." He lunges for my lips. "Please tell me you can juggle."

I want to cry. Literally fucking cry. He gets me.

Panting for him without realizing it, I say, "Take me back to bed, Henry. Make love to me this time."

His smile fades. The emotion is palpable, charging the air around us. "I love you, Elle," he whispers.

"I know that now. And you'll never have to prove it to me again. For as long as I live, Henry." I brush my hand over the side of his head, feeling the silky golden strands between my fingers. "But I will spend the rest of my life doing everything I can to prove my love to you."

HENRY

Never in a million years had I expected today to turn out like this. I'd hoped that Elle might accept my apologies for my outburst at the game last weekend, the best outcome involving us shaking hands and agreeing to meet again.

But Elle, true to her eccentric nature, got the truth out of me and then proposed marriage. Not exactly how I'd envisioned it happening for me.

Hey, gotta respect a woman who knows what she wants. Still, I can't help but feel concerned for her.

Do I want her? Hell yes.

Do I want her for the rest of my life? Hell to the yes.

Do I want her anywhere near my emotional Chernobyl of a family? Ohellno. Not when she's got so many other things to worry about.

"What's the matter, Henry?" she says as I lay my naked body between her thighs, my mind whirling with a million thoughts. I've never made love to a woman. I've fucked, screwed, and nailed. Not once have I ever done this.

Oh hell. My knees are shaking.

I smile. "You've got me all nervous."

"Do I now?" She kisses me, sweeping her tongue over my bottom lip.

It's not easy for me to say how I feel. I am used to hiding my emotions—in front of family, on the field, and certainly when in the public eye at family events. Stiff upper lip, charming smile, nice words—any of those I can do. But talking about my feelings? That's not my thing.

I will have to show her how I feel.

ELLE

Henry's strong, hard body blankets mine, and I couldn't be more turned on in this moment. He's all heart, I've realized, and now his is pounding against my chest. He's tense from head to toe, and his cock is harder than hell, the head nudging at my entrance.

I can tell that whatever's happened between us just now changed things. There's love between us and in what we're about to do.

Staring into his eyes, I plant a gentle kiss on his sensual lips and rock my hips into him.

He answers with a slow kiss back and then trails his lips and scruff down the side of my neck, leaving behind deliciously warm tingles.

It feels so good that I hardly notice his shaft isn't where I want it.

He kisses his way down to my breasts and cups

the left one in his rough hand while his tongue circles my taut nipple on the right. I know he's kissed my breasts before. I know he's kissed every inch of my body, but this is the first time I feel like he's tapped into my erogenous superhighway.

He begins sucking on my nipple, and the sensation tugs at my g-spot. My entire core begins to throb and ache for him, making me wetter than I've ever been.

How does he do that?

I cup the back of his head, digging my fingertips into his soft, dirty blond hair, my body squirming involuntarily.

He switches sides and begins sucking on the other nipple while sliding his hand down, over my waist and hip and then between my legs.

I gasp the moment his thick finger channels between the folds and finds my entrance.

"Mmmm…you're so wet," he says.

"All for you," I whisper.

He thrusts his fingers into me, and I buck.

"Oh God," he says, "you feel so warm and silky." His mouth moves down lower, and I feel his tongue sliding over my c-spot. He doesn't need to do this because I'm ready to burst and craving the kind of orgasm I can only get from his thick shaft pushing my limits. But it feels so good, I'm unable to stop him. Or speak. Or think or—

He starts sucking my clit and thrusting deep with those fingers, triggering an explosion of euphoria. My body tenses as the waves of wonderful contractions pound through my core and radiate outward.

"Fuck, fuck." I grab fists full of blanket and my head whips from side to side while his mouth and tongue and fingers literally rip the orgasm right out of this space so deep inside me that it feels like it comes from a different plane of existence.

After several long moments, the contractions melt away, leaving me limp and breathless. "Wow," I pant.

Henry wipes his mouth on my inner thigh, scratching me with his whiskers. I don't even care. I don't want to move. This feeling is just too good.

Henry moves over me, spreading my thighs with his large legs and planting his hands to the sides of my head. He takes no time positioning his cock and thrusts deep. I'm wet and relaxed, but my bud is sensitive. His shaft feels harder, thicker, and longer than ever because I can feel every inch of his dick inside me, sliding and thrusting.

I realize he's fucking me bare, and it ignites me all over again. The scorching arousal deep inside is almost agonizing as he stares at me with those sexy green eyes and pumps his hips. I open my legs wider, wanting him deeper, and run my hands behind him to cup his hard ass. I love how it feels as those smooth round muscles are flexing beneath my palms. I love the feel of his balls slamming against me. Nothing has ever felt so good, so right.

Henry begins moving faster, hammering his thick cock into me over and over again. I'm so close to coming, but I want to wait. I want to come as he ejaculates inside me.

He lowers his head and kisses me hard and then pushes the force of his body into me. His entire body tenses, and he lets out a deep, animalist groan that does me in. I let go and melt into him, feeling the tip of his cock pressing into my womb, the base of him putting the right amount of pressure on my throbbing bud. The orgasm tears through me, gripping me with hard waves of wicked pulses. I moan and pant, but I want to scream. The orgasm is tortuously good, lighting up every muscle with hot spasms.

As I'm coming, he makes small little thrusts with his cock, flooding me with the silky heat of his cum. I open myself wider for him, never wanting the moment to end. Being with him like this is like a drug, and I know I'll never tire of it.

Several moments pass, and I feel his body relax, but he stays inside me, propping his body on his elbows. Still, he's heavy and I love it.

"That was amazing." He plants a lingering kiss on my neck.

"I have no words," I pant.

"That's a first."

"Just rest. Because I need you to do that again as quickly as possible."

CHAPTER TWELVE
ELLE

Henry and I spend the next few hours making love, eating, and hydrating. He's insatiable in the sack and I can't help thinking that it's because he's got all of this pent-up emotion inside him. Either way, these were the best three hours of my life. I can't remember feeling so happy or satisfied or euphoric.

No, I'm not so worried about getting pregnant because the probability is low at this particular point in my cycle, but I do note that I need to get on the pill quickly. I don't ever want to go back to just screwing Henry. I want every time with him to be like this. Close. Intimate. And deliciously raw.

Speaking of raw…

"Wow. You really rode me hard." I chuckle, lying next to him with my head on his bare chest. He's well-endowed, so it's probably going to take a day or two for me to recover.

"I was making up for lost time," he says with a tinge of seriousness in his voice.

I lift my head and look at him. "What's the

matter?" He has to know there's a way to fix this deal he's made with his father. I've already come up with several solutions, but the first and most obvious step is to go and see the man. I'm not afraid of him. And despite what Henry's said, I have to believe the guy loves his son. This leverage move—using my mother to get Henry to give up his dream of the NFL—was merely an opportunity to get what he wanted. But I find it difficult to believe that Henry's father really would've let my mother just die like that. No, it was a game of chicken and Henry flinched. At least, that's what I want to believe.

"I'm worried for you," he says.

"Why me?" I run my hand over the side of my Henry's head, dragging my fingernails through the soft strands. I love his messy, unkempt hair. It's just too sexy.

"If you marry me, they'll try to control you, Elle. They've done it with my sisters and my new brother-in-law."

"How?" I ask.

"Chewy, my older sister's new husband, is from Nigeria. His parents are schoolteachers, so my father offered to build two new wells and a school in their village so there's room for more children."

"That actually sounds kind of generous of your dad," I point out.

"My brother-in-law thought so, too, but running the school and hiring more teachers requires money. Guarding the village requires money. So my father told my sister Michelle that the funding would be there as long as they needed it if she took over Claire's role in the company next year."

"I'm not following?"

"Claire's my older sister. She's been running the charities and public relations side for four years, but he wants her to take over some of the expansions outside of the oil business. He needs someone to take Claire's spot."

I give Henry's words some thought. "Honestly, it sounds to me like your father trusts you guys and just wants you running things. I'm not sure it's entirely evil of him."

"Oh, that part isn't evil, but it's the hard ultimatums he gives us. 'Do as I ask, or you'll be cut off. From all of us.'"

"Oh." I see now. He uses their love against them. "That's not very nice."

"No," Henry agrees. "It's not. And my mother is just like my dad, which is why you need to stay far, far away from them. They always start out seeming charitable, but they're really ruthless, bloodthirsty sharks. They use money to control everyone."

Walking away and telling them to shove their money is an option for Henry and his siblings, of course, but if they're threatened with losing their family, too? That's a bit harsh. Add to that, making the money about something that's bigger than only one person—like clean water and schools for a poor village in Nigeria—it would take a very heartless person to walk away from that.

"It's kind of sad, Henry."

"What?"

"I think that if your parents didn't force all of you to be their little minions, you'd probably want to work for them. You, for example. Were you planning to play football forever?"

"No. I really just want to play as long as my body will let me, but that isn't very long."

"See. The blackmail is completely unnecessary. And you know, I've reviewed over three hundred case studies on companies and their psychological underpinnings. Ultimately, their longevity and success is tied to the culture. And culture, of course, is really just another way of saying that a group of people have collectively agreed on how they feel about something—whether it's good or bad, a positive force in their lives or a negative one. From there, the behavioral norms and rules are established, including systems of reward and hierarchy. It's all very fascinating. But at the end of the day, running a company is astoundingly simple. You hire capable people and then you work to raise them up as high as they can go. But the moment you use threats and blackmail to control people, you've created a prison."

Henry gives me a strange look. "I thought you were a physics major."

"I am a woman of many interests, Henry. I've read over three thousand textbooks, lectures, and case studies in the areas of business, psychology, art, history, computer science, agriculture, and biology. Oh, and I know just about everything there is to know about making Twinkies—it was a phase when I was eight. But I've taken over eighty online classes and have completed the work of about thirty degrees."

"So why don't you have any?"

I shrug. "I find the pace of a classroom much too slow since the rate I can process information is fairly robust."

"Jesus, I didn't know dating a human computer could be so hot. You got a laptop handy, 'cause I think I'd like to have a three-way."

"Ha!" I slap his arm. "Funny."

"Oh, no. I'm not joking." He rolls me onto my back and pins me down. "Talk nerdy to me, baby. Do some math out loud." He kisses me.

"Stop it," I giggle. "You're making fun of me."

"Nope. I'm just your fan. Especially now that I know I'll never have to Google again, I think I will definitely agree to be your husband. But on one condition."

"Are you discarding the football wedding?" I ask.

"No. That stands. So make it two conditions."

"What?"

"When the time comes, we only invite our closest friends—okay. And your family, too, I suppose."

Ah. Meaning, he doesn't want his parents there.

"I am not afraid of your parents, Henry." I'm sure there's a reason for how he feels, but his father sounds like your stereotypical power monger. They are driven by fear—fear of losing, fear of being unimportant, fear of being powerless. I know exactly how to crack that kind of coconut. You appeal to their need for control. *And if that doesn't work, maybe I can win him over with some juggling.*

"You should be afraid, Elle," Henry says. "Which is why I'm going to do everything in my power to keep them away from you."

Oh, boy. Then you're really going to be pissed after I go visit your dad Monday morning. But there is no way in hell I'm letting Henry give up his dream without a fight. Besides, I think I owe this man, Henry's father, a thank-you for everything he's done for my mother, and it's the perfect excuse to pay him a visit.

Still pinned beneath Henry, I lift my head and peck his lips. "Two plus two is four. Four plus four is eight. Eight plus—"

"Oh, Elle..." He starts nuzzling my neck. "Don't stop, baby. Don't stop."

After a quick dinner—Chinese takeout since we were both tired—Henry dropped me off at the hospital so I could check on my mother once more and get my car before heading home to feed Mr. Nucleus, II. Henry gave me the longest, most passionate kiss in the car I'd ever had. And if it weren't for two very important people I needed to worry about—him and my mother—I could've stayed there all night, enjoying the fullness of his lips, the roughness of his jawline, and the feel of his enormous arms wrapped around me.

I wished him luck at his game in Indiana tomorrow and told him I'd be there cheering in spirit. I then went up to my mother's room to find that my father had gone home to shower and change. My sister, Lana, was there reading *Cat in the Hat* aloud. It was a tip I'd read in a study that reading something that one can associate with positive memories helps boost happy brain waves.

Anyway, the nurse said her vitals were strong and her blood work came back looking good, which means her body is responding to the medicine and getting ready to fight a war. I read the studies on the drug, so I concur, but even I don't know what will happen. This is the part of life that all of the smarts in the world cannot help. It's human will and a million different external variables all rolled together. Fate, chaos, luck—people call it many things, but I simply see it as the reason that sometimes things happen when they're not supposed to. And sometimes things don't happen when all of the right ingredients are present. Not everything in the universe has a rhyme or reason, though many scientists would argue against that. Sometimes you just *gotta* have faith.

Saturday, I spend most of the day with my mother and we watch Henry play on my smartphone. "See, Mom, there he is right here," I point to the dot among many dots on my screen, "ripping off that guy's head. He's awesome, right?" I admit, the man knows how to use the force of his mass to create a desired outcome. The delicious soreness between my legs is proof of that.

"So are you two official now?" she asks.

"Yeah. Very," I say, but I'm hesitant to tell her about my crazy proposal. I know she'll worry and say I'm too young and the last thing she needs is to worry.

"I'm happy you've found someone," she mutters and dozes off with a smile on her face.

"I am, too, Mom," I whisper. Because for the first time in my life, I feel like everything's going to be okay. *Just don't screw it up, Elle.*

Sunday, Mr. Nucleus and I meet Tassie at the dorms and I clean out my closet. She's completely sad that I'm leaving school until I tell her that Henry and I have decided to be together and that I asked him to marry me.

"I told you!" She squeals, jumps, and claps. "You two are perfect together! Ha! When's the wedding? Can I be maid of honor? Or maybe your minister? I'll get my license online! I've always wanted to marry someone."

I pick up my sweet little kitten, who's burring his face in my purse on the bed, and stroke him between the ears. He's the most laid-back kitten I've ever seen. You can cuddle him all day long and he won't complain.

"I know we're already parents," I say jokingly, "but we are a long way from getting married. I just wanted him to know that I'm dead serious about him being the one."

"Still," Tassie sucks in a breath and whooshes it out, a dreamy look in her eyes, "it's so sweet."

"I thought *you* were against marriage."

"I am for me, but there's no doubt in my mind that Henry and you are good for each other," she says.

"Which is why I have to figure out how to get him back in the game."

"I thought *you* hated the fact he plays football," she says.

"I didn't hate it. I simply didn't see him as relationship material—he seemed way too committed to beer and sports. But then he left the frat and gave everything up to save my mother. I just don't think you get better ingredients for love than that."

"But you do love him. Right, Elle?"

"Yeah. I mean, it sort of snuck up on me, but I've never seen a sexier guy or met anyone quite like him." Honestly, I can't seem to contain how much love I feel inside for this man. "That's why I'm going to talk to his father and try to work something out." In my mind, this has an easy solution. Let Henry play football for four or five years, and then Henry will likely want to work in the family business.

"I don't know, Elle. I've heard some of the things Henry's said in casual conversations when I've stayed with Hunter at the man-pad. Henry's dad sounds like a complete bastard."

"I'm sure he is, but Henry's delusional if he thinks I'm going to just sit back and do nothing." After all, Henry gave up everything for me. Why wouldn't I try to help him?

There's genuine worry in Tassie's blue eyes. "I guess you have to do what you think is right, but be careful, Elle. I've heard rumors about Henry's family."

"Like what?" I ask.

"That people who've tried to challenge them end up missing—stuff like that."

"Really? No way."

She shrugs. "They're the richest family in the state. I doubt that they got that way by playing nice."

"Of course, but murder? Sounds like bullshit to me." I hope.

"Still, be careful. And call me afterwards. Tell me how it went."

"You'll be the first to know."

෨ ෬

Monday morning, I pull my hair into a neat bun and put on black slacks, a white blouse with red pinstripes, and a matching red tie. Mr. Nucleus II and I are staying at my parents' house again, so I'm back in my old bedroom. I text my father and let him know I'll stop by the hospital later and bring him some nonhospital food; then I hit the road. It's an hour drive into Houston, and I want to get there early because I don't have an appointment.

But I have a plan.

I park on the street and enter the enormous skyscraper's lobby, quickly noting the sterile atmosphere and lack of smiles. People are shuffling by the turnstiles with card readers, past a security desk, not one happy face to be had on any of them.

"Hi, I'm here to see Chester Walton," I say to the burly security guard with a giant silver mustache.

"Your name?"

This is going to be a risk, but there's no other way for me to get in to see such a busy man. "Just tell him that Henry's fiancée is here."

The man gives me a look. "You're...Henry Walton's fiancée," he says with extreme skepticism.

"Yep."

The man takes a breath, picks up the phone, and dials. "Hi. I have a young woman here to see Mr. Walton. Says she's Henry's fiancée." He bobs his head. "Thank you." He hangs up the phone and then reaches for a visitor's badge. "Take the last elevator on the left. It will go straight to the top floor."

I hadn't expected it to be this easy. "Thanks." I go through the badge scanner and take the turbo elevator all the way to the forty-fifth floor. The moment the doors open, I notice the lifeless ambiance extends here, too. It's like they hired Scrooge as their interior decorator.

"May I help you?" says an older woman with glasses and brown hair. She smiles, but I can tell she doesn't mean it. She's got a sad, defeated look in her eyes.

"I'm here to see Mr. Walton."

"And you are?" she asks.

"Megan, tell the pilot we'll be leaving at two—" A large man emerges from his office, and I know right away he is Henry's dad. The broad shoulders, the nose, and height are unmistakable Walton traits.

"Who's this?" Henry's father looks me over like he'd sooner spit on me than speak to me directly.

"Uhhh..." The assistant swallows hard like she knows something bad is about to happen.

"Elle." I stick out my hand. "I'm Elle Williams."

He stares blankly for a moment. "Ah. You're Henry's little charity case—the one with the dying mother."

Thanks for the sensitive touch, buddy. "Yes. That's me, but we're hopeful she's going to come through this. Actually, that's why I'm here. I know you're busy, but do you have a moment? It's extremely important. It's about Henry."

"What did he do now?"

"I promise if you'll just give me a few minutes, I'll be out of your hair."

With a snarl on his lips, he steps aside and holds out his arm, gesturing for me to go inside his office.

Why do I feel like I've just been invited into a kraken cave?

I smile politely. "Thanks."

He follows me in, shuts the door, and goes over to his desk, taking a seat. "You have sixty seconds. What can I do for you?"

Ah, yes. The control freak. I try to keep in mind that men like this think of themselves as gods. I am not here to challenge that or change him. I'm here to get what I need for Henry.

"Thank you. That's very generous," I say. "Everyone knows how busy you are, so first, I'll start out by saying how grateful I am for what you've done for my mother. It's not every day a stranger takes their time and money to help someone like that."

"We help people all the time. Haven't you ever heard of the Walton Charitable Trust?"

"I have. Out of the five point two billion dollars of net income you brought in last year, you donated five million."

He makes a circle with his hand, urging me to wrap it up.

"Yes, so, I'm asking you to reach into that generous heart of yours and give one more time to someone who isn't a stranger. Please, let Henry off the hook. His dream is to go pro, and I think not having that chance is the kind of thing that could ruin him. And I find it difficult to believe that you've worked so hard to give him everything just so he'll be miserable his entire life."

"So that dipshit son of mine really thinks this will work? Sending some…" he makes a sour face and his green eyes wash up and down my body, "some poor little nerdy girl to beg on his behalf?"

Wow. What a jerk. But fine. I can take it. "Henry has no idea I'm here, sir. But if you could see what this ultimatum of yours has done to him, I think you'd—"

"I *think* you can turn right around and remove your skinny little ass from my office. No one here gives a shit about what you think."

This guy is so offensive. I might need to challenge him to a game of chess and put him in his place. "Well, Henry cares."

"Henry's a child."

What? "He's a man. A good man. And I'm sure despite your caustic language, you must've had something to do with that."

"He's a retarded pussy who likes to play with balls."

Whoa. Okay. That's about enough. "You don't talk about my fiancé that way. And calling anyone a retard is just plain insensitive. No wonder he doesn't want you at the wedding."

Henry's dad laughs. "Wedding? Whose?"

"Mine and Henry's. We're engaged."

He shakes his head with disgust. "What did my bonehead son of mine tell you, huh? That he loves you? And you believed him? You're a lot dumber than you look, sweetie, if you dropped your panties for that old line."

I literally want to throw up in this man's face. He's just that disgusting.

"Henry loves me. I love him. I don't need you to approve or—"

He stands from his exec chair and plants his hands on his desk. "Henry is already engaged. You've been suckered, Elle. He's marrying Candice right after he graduates."

I'm a bit stunned because, obviously, he's lying. Only, he doesn't sound like he's lying.

He continues, "Now, I'll give you ten seconds to leave my office, or I'll have you arrested for trespassing. Oh, and if you interfere with Henry marrying Candice, not only will I make sure your mother's treatment stops, I'll make sure your family is thrown out on the streets."

I gasp in horror. "You can't do that."

"Sweetheart," he begins loosening his tie and unbuttoning his shirt, "I can do anything I like."

Ohmygod. Is he taking off his clothes? Why's he taking off his clothes? What the fuck?

I start backing toward the door, wondering how this situation turned all rapey on me. "You're a monster," I whisper.

"Yeah. So I've heard," he says. "Now unless you want to see where Henry gets his impressive size from, I suggest you leave." He begins unzipping his slacks, and I bolt from the room, slamming the door behind me.

I'm in tears. "What the hell?"

"It's eleven o'clock," says his assistant, who's at her desk, looking at me with pity. "Naked yoga," she explains. "Eleven o'clock sharp every morning. He waits for no man. Or woman. Or assistant."

I cringe. "Oh, God. Really? That's just wrong." But I'm relieved that Henry's dad isn't Chester the Molester.

He's just a really big asshole.

She nods. "It gives new meaning to the word *dictation.* That's for certain."

Off the top of my head, he's breaking at least twenty laws. "As your boss, he can't do that. You should talk to a lawyer."

"Honey, he owns all the lawyers in this town. Best not make that man angry."

I let out a breath and run my hand over my hair. This guy isn't simply cruel, he's insane.

Wait. It hits me like a ton of bricks. Filled with jealousy. *Henry's already engaged?* No. I don't believe it. I won't believe it.

I look at Megan. "Does Henry have a fiancée?"

She hesitates for a moment and then gives me a nod. "Candice."

My heart fills with heavy, toxic tar. "For how long?"

"I don't know, miss. I think since they were in high school."

I nod slowly, trying to let that poison sink in. I wouldn't trust one word coming from Chester the Molester's mouth, but this woman? She has nothing to gain from lying to me.

"Is there really a wedding planned for next spring?" I rasp out.

With sympathy in her eyes, she slides an envelope across her desk. "June. This is the proof from the printer."

Seeing the eggshell-colored paper with the gold calligraphy literally makes me want to retch. How could Henry lie to me like this?

"Thanks," I say and stagger toward the elevators. My mind has officially been blown, but not in a good way.

What am I going to do next?

CHAPTER THIRTEEN
HENRY

I'm sitting in class Monday morning when my cell starts buzzing away. My English professor is a complete ballbuster when it comes to electronics, so I ignore the thing. After three rounds of vibes, I begin to wonder if it's an emergency. Plus, I haven't heard back from Elle this morning.

I get up quickly and exit into the hallway. To my surprise, the texts are from Tassie. I didn't even think she had my number.

Tass: *This is Tass! WTF, Henry!*

Tass: *Watch your back.*

Tass: *Gonna hurt u! Baaaad.*

Huh. That's weird. I wonder if someone has hacked her phone. I dial Tass, but it goes straight to voice mail.

"Hey, Tass. What's going on? Call me back."

I put the phone in my jeans pocket and head for the classroom when my phone rumbles for attention. I take a look at the screen.

What the…? It's a giant middle finger emoji.

Tass: *U R dead meat!*

What is going on? I toggle through my contacts and call Hunter, who's probably in class, too.

"Henry, man," Hunter answers right away.

"Dude, what's going on?" I ask.

"You mean that Tassie has vowed to castrate you?" Hunter says, completely serious.

"That sounds like it."

"I can't say I'm in a different place, man. Elle's mother is practically dying, and you cheated on her?"

"Hunt, I have no clue what you're talking about."

"You're telling me you didn't get engaged to Elle, but you're already engaged to some other chick?"

What? "I'm not engaged. Well, I am now—to Elle, but—"

"Elle went to see your dad, and he told her all about your wedding next summer."

At first, I find it difficult to understand what Hunter has just said. Then it clicks, and I go to worry mode. Then it sinks in a little further and I go to full-on pissed off. I specifically told Elle to stay away from my parents. They're toxic.

"Why would Elle do that?" I seethe.

"Why would you play her like that, man?" Hunter asks.

"You know what? Fuck you, Hunter. You should know me better than that by now."

"So you're not marrying some other chick next summer."

"No!" I bark.

"But, dude, Elle says there's a wedding date and everything. She saw the invitations."

"Whatthefuck?" My father has crossed the line this time. I've given up football and my future. I've let him push me to get everything he wanted. But I'm done. Done.

Of course, then my mind starts telling me who I'm dealing with. This is Chester Walton. There is no limit to how hard he'll fight to get something. That includes using Elle's mother's treatment as leverage. I could try for a football contract and get the advance, then renege on my deal with my dad after I have the money to pay for Elle's mother's treatment, but there are two issues. Any deal I sign with a team will be public. My father will find out. And, if by some miracle, I was able to keep the deal a secret, the moment I break the promise to my dad, he'll disown me. He'll do everything in his power to keep my sisters away from me and keep Elle's mother from getting any help.

I feel trapped in a fucking nightmare. One that has no end in sight.

I groan out a breath. "Hunter, man. I'm fucked. My father isn't going to let me live my life."

"What about Elle?" he asks.

I am beyond pissed that she went behind my back and meddled. There are no words for how betrayed I feel. Still, I owe it to her to at least listen to what she has to say.

"I don't know, Hunt. Maybe it's just not going to work out. Because I can't win with my father. I can't throw her mother under the bus. I can't see a way out of this fucking mess. Any advice?"

"Yeah, don't go anywhere near Tassie."

&ipsilon; &ipsilon;

As usual, Elle has shut me out. I swear, I'm going to spank her if she does that again. Because it's childish to block someone every time there's a problem. Of course, I would never really hit a woman—but damn, I want to paddle her.

I pull up to her house, which is two hours from campus, and see her white car out front. I park, go up to the door, and ring the bell. Of course, she's not answering.

"Hey, Elle!" I yell up at the windows. "Get your ass to the door! We gotta talk."

Nothing happens.

"Fine. But you broke a major rule with me. You went behind my back! So if you ever want to see me again, now's your chance."

The window flies open. "Shut up, you cheater!"

"I am not engaged to that troll, Elle. And you ought to be ashamed for even believing that."

"I saw the wedding invitations!"

"That's because my dad is psycho. I told you that. But did you listen to me? Did you trust me? No! You just march over there and fucked with things you don't understand, all because you think you're smarter than everyone else. Well, I have news for you, Elle. You do not know everything! But you sure as hell know how to ruin a good relationship and piss me off!"

I turn and head for my truck, hoping to Christ I don't lose it and punch something like a tree trunk, because, man! I am pissed. That woman has just gotten on my last nerve, and I've been trained to release my anger by plowing into shit. *Goddamn, when is practice?*

I get into my truck and start the engine.

"Henry!" Elle pounds on the glass to my side. "Where are you going?"

I lower the window. "Away from you. You don't want a boyfriend or a relationship, you want problems and puzzles to solve. I'm not your guy, Elle."

"Stop. Just tell me, who is Candice?"

"She's no one. And if I have to say more than that, then—"

"I believe you," she blurts out. "And I'm sorry I went to see your dad. I thought I could reason with him. I thought I could talk him into letting you go pro."

I laugh. "Reason with him? That man? No,

Elle." I shake my head. "You don't reason with my father. You just defend your territory, and he eventually wears you out."

"Yeah," she reaches through the window and places her hand on mine, "I get that now. I'm so sorry, Henry. He's awful."

"Yes. He is."

"Then let's go inside and figure something out. He can't keep doing this to you forever and there has to be another way to get my mom her treatment—donations or something."

"My dad owns the drug company, Elle. If I go back on my word, money's not going to help. He'll find a way to keep the medicine out of her hands."

"Then we have to find a way around him. There has to be something. Otherwise, he'll just keep using her to get what he wants. He even used it against me."

"How?"

"He said if I got in the way of you and Candice, he'd pull treatment from my mom."

"That son of a bitch." But now Elle's been pulled into this, and I know what happens when you go up against my dad. You lose. You suffer. And if that's not enough to make him feel vindicated, he'll go after more things you care about.

"I can't see you anymore," I say. "You don't need this in your life."

"Henry, just come inside. We can figure this out together."

"No. He's won. And I don't want to see you hurt."

"Henry, please—"

"Elle," I bark, "you're not calling the shots, and you can't think your way out of this."

"I'm not giving you up," she whispers with fragile calm in her voice, nearly breaking my heart.

I let out a slow breath. She has to hear me. She has to understand. "He's got you backed into a corner, Elle. You have to decide between your mother or me, and I know which one I'd choose."

"Please, Henry. Just come inside. If you don't want to figure a way out of this, then at least don't end things by driving away angry. I can't take any more heartache than I've already got."

She places her soft hand on my arm. "No one's home."

I look into her big brown eyes and drink in those pouty little lips. It's hard for me to say no to that. "I don't think it's a good idea."

She cocks her head. "Everything's so messed up, I just don't think it matters anymore." She walks away, and I see a heaviness in her steps. I want to protect her from this fucking nightmare of my family, who's more like the mob than parents. She disappears into her house, and I sit there for ten minutes, trying to think of a way through this. There are no plays, no defenses, no Hail Marys. I lost this game the moment I was born.

I look up at her window, wanting her so badly I

can taste it.

"Fuck it." I grab my keys from the ignition and exit my car. What's one last time?

ELLE

I'm standing inside the entryway of my house, eyes closed, facing the front door. I don't know how I've managed to make this situation worse, but I have. Because Henry's right; I don't know everything. And I can't think my way out of this.

Dammit. If I'd just kept my mouth shut and listened to Henry.

I open my eyes, staring intently at the front door. *Come on, Henry, don't end things like this.* I hope once he calms down, we can figure this out together. There has to be some sort of leverage he can use against his father so we can be left to live our lives.

Come on, Henry. I clench my fists, willing him to walk through that door.

Ten minutes pass, and he doesn't, which makes me think that he doesn't believe in us, that maybe he didn't really mean it when he once said that we could conquer the fucking world together.

I turn to go into the kitchen and make myself some tea or vodka—I'm not sure—when the door flies open.

My heart swells and my breath catches. *Henry...*

He rushes toward me and grabs me by the waist, simultaneously turning my body and lifting me. His lips are on my mouth and he pushes my back to the wall. His movements and kisses are frantic and needy. I'm instantly turned on by the feel of his hard cock pushing through his pants into me.

"I love you," he pants between steamy kisses.

"I love you, too." I wrap my arms around his neck and slide my tongue past his soft lips. He has no idea what he does to me. Sexually, mentally, and in my heart—he's won everything. Which makes it impossible to believe there's no way through this. Sadly, however, the only solution my mind comes up with is marrying Henry now, before anything else happens, and then exposing Henry's father if he pulls the treatment for my mother. Of course, that would just drag Henry through the mud and we'd forever be hounded by the media, including my mom. It's a terrible, horrible idea. But if it means I get Henry and she has her chance to live, then what else can I do?

Henry won't want that. And he won't forgive me if I go out on my own and "fix" things again.

I push away my thoughts and focus on the man between my thighs, grinding against me, kissing me with complete abandon, and panting my name.

He drops me for a moment, his mouth never leaving me, and tugs down my sweats. I kick them off the rest of the way while he pops the top button on his jeans and yanks down his pants mid-thigh, exposing his hard cock. I take one look at it—the tight pink skin, the soft velvety head, the impressive length—and the only thing I want is to take him in my mouth. I look up at him for a moment and a smile creeps over my wet lips. Oh, yeah. I'm totally doing this. Not only is it a fantasy of mine, because I've never done it before, but nothing inspires a man more—so I hear. Maybe he'll come up with a brilliant idea in the process.

A miracle blow job. My best idea today.

I lower myself to my knees and grip him firmly in my hand.

"Elle, you don't need to do tha—oohhh…" he moans as I take the length of him in my mouth, swirling my tongue over the salty tip. His smell is musky and all male, something I'm not used to, but I remember once reading how the animalistic parts of our brains still respond strongly to pheromones whether we realize it or not. Which explains why as I'm sucking him in, pushing the head of his cock all the way to the back of my throat, I'm the one who feels aroused. One flick of my c-spot and I'll be sailing to O-land.

Henry threads his strong fingers through my hair and begins pumping his hips in time to the movements of my mouth. His pants and deep groans urge me on, making me take him as far as he can go.

I wrap my hand around the base of his shaft so he feels me on every inch of him. I want him to remember how good I make him feel and that we're a match in every possible way.

Henry pants my name, and I go faster, knowing he's about to come. My clit is throbbing and my core is aching to come with him.

Henry suddenly pulls away. He jerks me to my feet and spins me around to face the wall. "Spread your legs," he demands, his voice husky.

I step my feet apart, and he snakes a strong arm around my waist. I know what's coming, so I brace my hands against the wall.

He's taller than me, so he pushes between my shoulders, bending me over further. I hold my breath, waiting for his delicious penetration to release the sinful pressure screaming inside me.

A moment passes. Then a moment more. My brain is in this lustful fog, but I can hear a quiet buzzing. A cell phone?

"Hello?" I hear Henry's voice say.

I straighten out and spin around to face him. "Ohnoyoudidnt, Henry. Tell me you did *not* just answer the phone in the middle of sex." *Really, really hot dirty sex.*

He holds up a finger to silence me, listening to whoever's talking. "Police? Why? What do they want?" He bends over and pulls up his jeans with his shaky hand.

"That can't be right," he says, his face growing ghost white. He listens some more and then lets out a "Fuck."

I can tell this is bad, bad news. I can see it on his face. As far as he's concerned, I'm not even here.

"Okay. I'll be there as soon as I can," he says and slides his cell into his jeans while I quickly pull on my sweats.

"What happened?" I ask. "Who was that?"

His eyes glazed over, he just sort of stares at the wall. "That was Hunter."

"And?" I'm thinking something happened to his teammates.

"The corporate jet went down over the Gulf of Mexico. The plane's missing."

I gasp. *Oh no. Oh no.* "Who was in it, Henry?" I ask, and a tiny horrible part of me hopes it was his bastard of a father, but I quickly push back on myself. As bad as that man is, I don't wish him dead, not that the world wouldn't be a better place, but because I don't want Henry to lose his dad. I don't want Henry to suffer like that.

Henry blinks. "All of them."

"All of who, Henry?"

"My entire family. Even Michelle, who's supposed to be in Africa."

I cup my hands over my mouth. "Oh, God." I don't know what else to say.

Henry's face turns a shade of red I've never seen on a person before. "That fucking bastard. He did this. They wouldn't be on the plane if it weren't for him."

I want to touch Henry and hug him or say

something, but I can tell he needs his space. "That bastard better be dead, because if he's not, I'm going to kill him." He reaches for the door.

"Wait. Where are you going?"

"To my parents' house."

"I'll come with you."

"To do what, Elle? You've got enough on your plate. I'll be fine."

I blink at him. "You're in shock. This is horrible. You shouldn't be alone."

"Elle," he gives me a harsh look, "I've been alone my entire life. I'll be fine."

"But I—"

"You need to focus on your mother. I'll call you later."

He rushes out and drives away in his SUV. I know why he's pushed me away—he doesn't want me to see him break down or cry or whatever's going to happen next. And while I want to respect his space, I feel like chasing after him. I really want to be there for him.

Who are you kidding? You'll just make a mess of everything. Because if I'm honest with myself, I really don't know how to help him. I feel impotent and frustrated and frightened.

If anything, today has taught me that while I may be smart, I don't know everything. Especially how to help the man I love.

He said stay away. I should listen to him this time. But goddammit! That's not what I want.

CHAPTER FOURTEEN

I haven't heard from Henry much over the past few days, but the story is all over the news.

Billionaire Walton family missing.

Plane lost over Gulf of Mexico.

Russians plan to take over US Oil by taking out Walton family.

Okay, that last one is a tabloid story, and so is the latest headline from this morning, questioning why Henry was the only member of his family not on the plane.

Idiots. There is no limit to how low the media will sink.

"Any news, sweetie?" my mother mutters from her hospital bed, waking up from a morning nap.

"No." From the seat next to her, I shake my head at the television mounted to the wall across the room.

"You should go to him, Elle. He can probably use a good friend right now."

"If Henry wanted me around, he'd ask. He hasn't." We've just spoken for a few moments at a time. I ask how he's doing. He says okay. I ask what I can do to help. He says I should be with my mother.

"He's a man. Since when do they ask for help or say they need you?" she says.

I shrug. "I'll only want to meddle and help and I'll just end up making things worse." I don't want to create additional stress, especially after I really fucked things up before this all happened.

"You won't, honey. You're too smart for that."

I shrug. "I'm not so sure."

"Why would you say that?" my mom asks. "You're the smartest person I know."

"You have to say that. You're my mother."

"Elle, do you remember how you left us when you were thirteen to go live with your uncle Seymour?"

The circus uncle. How could I ever forget? It was the first time in my life I ever felt normal. "Yeah."

"Well, you left us because you knew exactly what you were doing. You knew that we were making bad choices and pushing you to the point of breaking. So you went to the only person who was crazy enough to listen to a thirteen-year-old and give her the space she needed, while protecting her. Smartest move you ever made."

Huh? She actually thinks that? "I'm shocked. All these years, I thought you were still mad about that."

"I was for a long time, but then I started to understand that we were always making your life about us. We saw you as some sort of invincible superwoman who could take on the world. But at the same time, we were treating you like a child who didn't know what was best for her. And we were wrong."

"I'm not following your point," I say.

"The point is you've always had a good head on your shoulders, and I'm not just talking about how smart you are. You come at problems from a completely different angle, and you're not afraid of making hard choices even when everyone else isn't thinking straight."

I don't see myself like that. I feel like I just get in my way—like I didn't see Henry for who he really was. I didn't see how I was hurting myself by not confronting my fears about my mother's health. I didn't listen to Henry about his father, because I believed I was smarter and knew better than him. I spend my mental energy in ways that create more problems than I solve.

"I keep getting in my own way," I mutter.

"Elle, baby, you're still so young. And you're allowed to make mistakes, but there's a time when you just have to trust yourself and your strengths. You're good at figuring things out and your passion is making things better. So go help Henry."

"I think I'll just call him instead—let him know that I'm here when he needs me."

"Don't be silly, Elle. Think about how you felt when I got sick. Now imagine that pain times ten. Henry's lost everyone."

I nod. She's right, but his resistance to my help isn't the only issue. "I think I'm afraid to go through more drama. Everything's been so rough lately."

"You can take it, Elle. You're my daughter, strong as...what's the strongest thing in the universe?"

I know what she's asking—diamonds, graphene, spider silk, carbyne—but there's only one answer in my mind.

"Love," I say.

She smiles. "Yes. Love. And I love you, Elle. Besides, I get to go home today. My vitals are stable, I'm eating and drinking regularly—I'm getting stronger every day."

"It's only been a week."

"I want to be in the comfort of my own home. We'll drive in as needed for doctor visits and tests."

This is great. "I'm so happy for you, Mom." This means Christmas at home. It's only ten days away.

"We have at least six months to go before we'll know if the treatment is working," she says. "But I have a feeling that it will."

I nod. "It has to. I need you."

Her big brown eyes tear up. "You love me, Elle, but you haven't needed me for a long, long time. Henry, on the other hand. I think you need him and he needs you."

I take a breath, trying not to cry while mulling over her points. "Did Tass call you?"

"Why do you ask?"

"Because I haven't really spoken much about Henry and all of a sudden you're pushing me to be by his side."

"Well, a little birdy may have told me that you asked him to marry you."

"Oh." But he can't marry me. Or he couldn't. Now everything is up in the air. I mean, if his dad is really dead, then there's nothing stopping us. That said, as much as we want to be together, we didn't want it to be like this. This is tragic. This is a giant sour pickle in our sweet, sweet relationship cake. "That Tassie. Can't trust her with anything."

"She just wanted to be a good friend."

"So you're not angry I didn't tell you?" I ask.

"I'm sure you didn't want to worry me. But I'll always worry no matter what you do. It can't be avoided."

I look down at my hands, shaking my head. "I worry about you, too, but I should've been honest."

"Forgiven. But right now I think you need to focus on Henry. Tassie said she's really worried about him."

"He says he's okay."

"Do you really believe that?" my mom says.

"No. But I'm trying to do what he's asked for once. He says he doesn't want me there."

My mother sighs. "Are you really serious about him, Elle?"

I nod once. "More serious than anything."

"Then go be with him."

It's not that simple. "There're issues."

"Sweetheart." She sighs again, this time with frustration. "That's what love is. Issues. One after another and another. But when you love someone, you just have to commit. And when bad things happen, you stand together and fight until you can't go any further. It's that simple. But if you're not ready to do that, then you're not ready for marriage because I promise there will never be a lack of reasons to quit. So you've got to have at least *one* good reason to stick it out: him." She blinks at me, her eyes threatening to tear. "You have to love *him*. And *you*. And what you make *together*. You have to believe in that one thing. Otherwise, it's not going to last."

I sit there trying to digest what she's saying. My heart knows she's right, but my brain tells me that I'm in a no-win situation. If his family survived, which I hope with all my heart they did, then I'm back to square one: Choosing between my mother's life or my love for Henry. If his family didn't survive, then there'll forever be a dark cloud hanging over our heads. Our relationship will feel like the tragic fruit of a tragic event, and neither of us can stomach that.

I bend my head and cover my face, whooshing

out an exasperated breath.

"What is it, Elle?" she asks.

"Everything keeps going the wrong way. And I can't fix it." I sob my words.

"Then don't try, Elle." She reaches for my back and makes tiny soothing circles over my shoulder blades the way only a mother can. "Just let all that go and be by his side."

"It's complicated." And I'm not about to tell her about Pervy Chester's ultimatum.

"Okay! Then it's complicated. But you fight for what you want, Elle. And you *commit* to what you need."

Her words are like a gallon of gasoline for my tired little engine that's run out of I-think-I-cans. I need to do more than try. I have to see it through to the end, until there is nothing left to give. Just like she's doing for us. Just like me, my sister, and my father are doing for her. We won't stop until we've won or there's nothing left to fight for.

I haven't done that for Henry. *For us.*

I stand up. "Okay. I'll go see him." I lean over and kiss her forehead. "Tell Dad I won't be home tonight. Don't want him to worry."

"Worry? About you? Never!" She smiles and the view makes my heart all tingly.

"Love you, Mom."

"Tell Henry that our thoughts are with him," she says. "And that if he needs anything, we're here."

I leave, surmising my mother knows more than she's letting on. Otherwise I'd be getting the lecture about how I'm too young to think of marriage. Instead, I get the Tammy Wynette "stand by your man" speech.

She's right, of course. I may be lacking experience, but I'm learning how to listen to the people who love me.

Dammit. I wish I'd started sooner.

HENRY

I sit in the family lawyer's office, my neck hot, my hands sweating as everyone is cleared from the room—Big Tom, a few of my dad's business partners, and an uncle who works at one of the drill sites that I never really see except for the occasional Christmas party.

Mr. Larson takes a seat, the buttons of his starched white dress shirt clacking against the edge of his desk because his belly protrudes so far.

"Now-a, Henry son," he says with a thick Texan accent, "I've asked you here today because there are several matters to discuss. Matters only for your ears." He shoves his reading glasses onto his pudgy red face and my first thought is that he's likely going to die of a heart attack before this conversation is over. I've seen Larson lurking at our summer fundraiser picnics, and he's not shy about his love of

BBQ ribs and beer.

"Fine," I say. "Just hurry up because I need to get back to my parents' house." I'd call it home, but there's no such thing in my world. There are just showplaces, impersonal assets where we spend time.

Regardless, a small army is camped out there, mostly people I've never met before, helping Megan—my father's assistant—and me with everything from press releases to pushing the Coast Guard not to call off the search, to keeping any vultures at bay. And the vultures are many. Business partners, investors, executives claiming my father owes them, and contractors waving around unpaid invoices for drilling crews. The line of heartless people who only care about their money is insane. At the very least, they could give me a week or two to focus on my family.

"Well, Henry, I've known your father a very long time—almost twenty years. And it's no secret that he likes to do things his way."

No. Really? "Yes. I am aware."

"Nor did the man trust many people—he was always going on and on about people tryin' to steal his fortune."

My mom's fortune, but whatever.

Larson continues. "That's the reason he didn't make the proper operational contingencies."

"What contingencies?"

He leans into his desk. "Henry, there's a will in place if he dies. There's also a living will in place that specifies what to do if he were ill and unable to speak on his own behalf about treatment. But there is nothin' in place to deal with a situation where he's missing. He's got over twenty companies and no one's manning the helm."

"So can't the teams at each of his companies just run things until we find him?" Because we have to find him. Him, my mother, and my three sisters. They can't all be dead. Life isn't that cruel, is it?

Larson shakes his head of thinning dark hair. "Your father kept strict control over everything, Henry. Only he has the authority to sign contracts, approve payments over one hundred thousand dollars, and make changes in the executive staff."

"Sounds like a hell of a lot of work."

"It is. But the crazy old hoot never slept."

I would feel bad for my father, except he chose to make things that way. "So what's going to happen, then?"

"Henry, as hard as this is going to be, we need to call off the search and file a motion with the court to declare your father dead."

Whatthefuck? "No. We're not giving up on finding them. That's ridiculous."

"Son, you need to see the big picture here." Larson holds up his thick arms like he's mimicking a goalpost. "Your family is likely gone, and without someone running those companies, they'll die a quick, painful death; all that money invested will go with them."

"If you're saying I should think about the money over my family's lives, then you're all crazy bastards." I seriously want to thump this guy over the head.

"Grow up, son. You're in the big leagues now. Do you know how many people with families depend on their paychecks? Your father's oil business alone has over ten thousand employees."

I hadn't thought about that, but I still won't throw away any chance of finding my family. They could be lost at sea in a raft. Time is of the essence.

Larson continues, "Now-a, I've got some connection with a few judges. We'll try to get them to rush through the paperwork."

"Why?"

"So everything can go to you, son. Your father left all his assets to his children and you're it."

I feel a huge lump build in my throat, and I can't choke it down. "I don't want to own it. I don't want to run his companies."

"Then sell it all. But that's going to take years. In the meantime, son, you'll need a team to help you run things. Now, I have some people that I can recommend—"

"No. We're not calling off the search."

Larson's cheap smile melts away. "Son, you'll have enough money in your pocket to search for them the rest of your life. But I'm not just going to leave empty-handed because your father was too stubborn to listen to me."

"Ah. Now I see. It's about the money." My hands tighten into fists.

"Everything is about money. Even your father had enough common sense to know that. As for you, if you're smart, you'll listen to me. I can make sure you're taken care of."

Asshole. Is that really what he thinks I'm worried about? Myself?

I suddenly realize that I'm just a guppy in a giant shark tank and they're all looking for a way to chew me up. I need someone I can trust. Someone smart who can sort through all of this to help me figure out what to do.

I need Elle.

I stand up. "I'll sleep on it. In the meantime, email me all this stuff you're talking about—the wills and a list of all his holdings."

"What do you need all that for? I told you everything you need to know."

Yeah, sure. "I want to see what I'm up against if I go with your plan."

"It's like I said, Henry, you simply gotta—"

"I'm guessing that your company bills us more than one hundred thousand dollars a month, right?"

He gives me a hard look. "We are on a retainer, yes. But we do a considerable amount of—"

"I'm also guessing you don't get paid if I don't go along with your plan, so if that's the case, then send me the information. All of it. Or I will find another lawyer to file those papers, and once I have control, my first act will be firing you."

He glares with his beady gray eyes. "I'll have Betsy, my assistant, send everything right over."

"Good man, Larson." *Vulture.* "I'll let you know my plans in the morning."

When I pull up to my parents' estate, there's a long line of new vans parked along the narrow street. They've been there for three days, and I don't expect them to leave anytime soon. I hit the remote on my visor and the iron gate slides open. Reporters crowd my SUV, tapping the glass with their microphones.

Morons. It's almost like they want me to run over them or punch them in the face just so they'll have something new to report.

I pull forward slowly, giving a quick wave to one of the security guards. Normally, my father has five guards, but the company's owner told me they now need ten just to keep up. People from everywhere, including every psychic in the state of Texas, wants in. It's insane.

I pull into the circular front driveway with a reflecting pool in the center and head for the door.

"Henry! Hey! It's me!" I turn my head and there's a petite blonde with large framed glasses yelling through the gate.

"Elle?"

She makes a little wave. The moment the reporters realize I know her, they mob her.

"Hey! Back off!" I storm toward the gate and tell the guard to reopen it.

"You did not just shove a microphone up my nose!" Elle pushes back on some skinny guy in a black tie. "Let's see how you like it!" She snatches the thing from his hand and smacks him square in the nose with it.

"Ow! That's assault," he whines.

"No, by law that's self-defense. You wanna see assault, bend over!"

I'm trying not to smile, but Elle is literally trying to grab his arm so she can turn him around. I'd better save the guy or he's going to end up being his own news story.

"Elle! Hey!" I get her attention and jerk my head to the side.

She sees the gate's open and that I'm waiting for her, but she still takes a moment to throw the microphone at the guy, who's now running away.

Thunk! She nails him right on the back of the head.

Ouch. That had to hurt.

"That'll teach you to attack a woman, you pig!" Elle stomps over, and I can see her nose is bloody. The cameramen keep their distance but continue filming.

"Jesus, what did he do to you?" Now I want to go after the guy and finish the job, though I love that Elle has no issue defending herself or humiliating a grown man on live TV.

Elle puts her hand over her nose. "It's just a little blood. I'm fine."

"Let's go inside and get you some ice." I look at the guard, who's just closed the gate. "Find out who that guy is. I want him arrested."

"No, Henry," Elle protests, "you've got enough to worry about." She looks at the guard. "But get his name; I might send him a package of bedbug-riddled PJs."

Jeez. "Is that a joke?"

"Infestation-O-Gram. They're your worst enemy's itchiest nightmare."

I cringe. "Remind me to never get on your bad side."

"Don't ever get on my bad side," she says in a deadpan.

"Funny." I open the front door for her and we step inside. "So why didn't you call and let me know you were coming?"

"I did. Five times, but it kept going to voice mail."

I slide the phone from my pocket and realize I'd put it on Do Not Disturb mode since I'd been in that meeting.

"Sorry about that," I say. "I switched it off. My cell doesn't stop ringing now."

"That's okay—"

"Henry!" Megan rushes to greet me at the foyer. "There's an issue with the San Antonio plant.

They're threatening a strike."

"Strike? For what?"

"Your father never signed the new union contract and the old one expires in a month."

"Then why are they walking out now?" I ask.

"Because the contract says that a new contract has to be in place thirty days before the expiration of the old one or they will consider it a termination and have the right to use up all of their unpaid leave."

"Fuck. Why didn't he sign it?" I ask.

Megan gives me a shrug like she doesn't know what to do.

Elle tugs on my arm. "I need to talk to you, Henry. Can we go somewhere private?"

I give her a look. "Just a minute, Elle. I have to go talk to the operations guys and see what our options are." I turn to Meg. "Find Frank Whatshisface and get him on the phone—"

"Tell the union leader to look at the force majeure clause in the contract," Elle says. "They'll have to wait for the agreement to formally expire or face a breach."

Huh? I give Elle a look.

She makes a flutter with her hand, like she's trying to hurry the conversation up. "Most contracts in the United States have a force majeure clause. It protects the parties from having to comply with terms of the contract if an act of God has occurred and impedes such execution."

I give her another look, not fully understanding.

"You know—if there's a natural disaster or something completely out of your hands like a chemical spill or another country declares war on us. Your father can't reasonably execute the contract renewal if his plane was hit by lightning, now can he? They'll have to wait. Not forever, of course, but it should buy you some time."

I knew Elle was the right person.

I turn to Meg and give her the nod. "Can you get Elle a bag of ice while you're heading that way?"

"Yes. Of course." Meg hurries off into the other room.

"Can we talk now?" Elle asks. "It's important."

"Actually, I was planning to call you tonight to talk over something important, too." I point upstairs. "Let's go somewhere more private."

She gives me a hesitant nod. "Okay. But no kissing. I don't want any distractions until I've said everything."

I'm intrigued. Add to that, the look in her brown eyes is sharp and determined, like she's on a mission. I might not be able to keep from kissing her.

"Then I'll lead the way," I say.

ELLE

I've run seventy-two scenarios through my head in

terms of how to tell Henry, in no uncertain terms, that I am not leaving. Not him. Not his side. Not until we have both concluded that our relationship can no longer thrive, which in my mind will never happen. As my mother said, at some point, you just have to commit and, come what may, you stick it out together.

Yes, his dad put us both in a horrible situation, but after thinking about what my mom said, I realized that Henry and I had failed to do one thing: Make a stand together. And that was our shortcoming: believing in us. We'd both allowed Henry's dad to kowtow us with fear. We'd allowed him to play by his rules.

Henry leads me into a study that smells like leather and cigars. I assume it's his father's. As for the house, it's a mansion—huge and impersonal with expensive-looking art on the walls, high ceilings, and the sort of furnishings you'd expect to see in a glossy new modern-day palace. I don't like it one bit. I love homes that are loved and lived in. Preferably with kittens.

Wearing a plain white button-down and jeans, Henry faces me with his arms crossed and leans his big body against the antique desk—circa 1920s from what I know about furniture. Which is a lot. Another phase that followed my Twinkie obsession.

"You want to go first?" he says.

"Yeah. I do. I want to say that I've made two mistakes—okay, three mistakes, counting the time I went to see your father. But I think it was the wrong choice for us to let your father put a wedge between us like that and to allow him to use my mother's life as leverage. So while I recognize he had backed us into a corner, I now see that we let it happen. We let him set the rules when we should've stood up to him together. As a team. Like you do on the field with your football bros. You don't always know how you'll win, but you get out there and you fight until the game is over. Well, we needed to be a team and we weren't. Which is why my second mistake was allowing you to push me away when clearly this is the worst moment of your life. So I'm here to say that I'm not going. And you can't make me, so don't try. And yes, maybe I'll make mistakes and bad choices, but I'm here for you whether you like it or—"

"Yes."

I stumble over my tongue. "Sorry?"

"Yes. I'm saying yes. You're right. I shouldn't have let my father win so easily. I shouldn't have pushed you away. And I need you. Like...really, really need you, Elle."

I blink. "Seriously?"

"I can't do this alone. It's too complicated, and without my father, the wheels are coming off the bus. I have no clue how to keep them on."

I can see he's trying to be strong with his words, but the pain in his eyes is unmistakable. And I know exactly what I would be doing if I were in this situation; I'd be in complete denial that anything has happened to my family. I would remain that way until I had reason to believe otherwise. So, logically, given how similar Henry and I are, I know that's exactly where he's at—trying to keep the wheels on the bus, just like he said.

Still, my heart weeps for him. This has to be tearing him up inside.

He continues, "Elle, I need someone I can trust to help me while I focus on finding my family."

"Of course. I'll help any way I can. What about school?" I ask.

He shakes his head. "I'm going to have to drop out. The companies my family owns have all come to a grinding halt because my dad was too stubborn and paranoid to rely on anyone for the big decisions." Henry begins to laugh and covers his face. "It's so damned ironic. My father's probably dead, and somehow he's still managed to keep me from living my life."

I touch his strong arm. "No, he hasn't, Henry. Just give me tonight, and I promise I'll find a solution."

"I don't even know the problems yet. The lawyer is supposed to send me a summary tonight. Plus he's pushing to call off the search and have my family declared dead, which would trigger the will to take effect and leave me owning everything."

"That sounds complicated. And…really expensive. Henry, you would lose half of the assets just trying to pay the inheritance taxes."

"Fuck. I hadn't even thought of that. But it explains why he wants to go that route. He and his friends probably want to buy pieces of our companies below market."

I can see the look on Henry's face. He's frustrated and pissed and tormented.

"Henry, you focus on finding your family. I'll take care of everything else. Okay?"

"I just need help finding another lawyer—one I can trust."

"I can do more than that, Henry. I have the equivalent of over thirty degrees. Still, I recognize that I'm no expert because I don't have experience in real-life applications. That said, I know enough to be dangerous and ask all the right questions so I can find capable people to do all of the work." I throw my arms around his neck. "Just trust in us."

His eyes soften, and he gives me a gentle kiss. "I'm lucky to have you, Elle."

And I'm lucky to have him. "Got time for a quickie?"

He chuckles. "Sadly, I don't."

"Awww...too bad, because I found my stash of birth control pills. Already been on them since last weekend." I'd originally got them after I started sleeping with Henry, but we ended things so quickly that we never made it past condoms.

"I'll be free in one hour," he says.

I smile, and it's because his face, though sporting the tired circles under his eyes, has a bit of a glow to it. I can already see his back is straighter and shoulders are squarer. I've lightened the load.

"I'm in love with you, Henry. I really am." And I'm in love with the idea of us, what we can accomplish.

"We can conquer the world together."

"My thoughts exactly! But why stop there?" I kiss him gently. "Because before I die, I am going to build a tele-transporter."

"You're so nerdy," he says. "I love it. Promise you'll talk math to me later?"

"Just as long as you show me your big jock muscles."

"Deal." He takes in a breath. "You know, I was expecting that when I fell in love, it would be like getting hit over the head with a giant hammer."

"And?"

"This wasn't like that. This is real. Not a movie or some big fantasy living in my head." His eyes gloss over a little.

"You're thinking about winning the Super Bowl, aren't you?"

He blinks. "How'd you know?"

I grin. "A wild guess."

"We're going to make a good team, Elle. I don't even mind having to give it all up as long as you're here with me."

Silly boy. I'm not going to let that happen. In fact, while we've been standing here, basking in the sweet triumph of our unlikely union, my brain has already done what it does best. It's given me an answer.

I got this.

CHAPTER FIFTEEN
HENRY

I haven't seen Elle since yesterday, but she's been texting me at all hours of the night with words of encouragement. *"I think I've got a solution, Henry! Can't wait to tell you all about it!"*

It's a new chapter for me. Having blind faith. In her, in me, and in the hope that the terror in my heart is for nothing. I can't handle thinking about having lost my family, especially my sisters. *Little Georgie. Oh, God.* I can't stomach the images of her screaming as the plane went down. She had to be so frightened, and I wasn't there for her.

I quickly push aside all of the emotions and morbid thoughts, locking them safely away for the time being. I've got to be strong. I've got to focus on finding them and not allowing thousands of people's lives to go to hell because of my father's incredibly stupid choices.

If I ever see you again, Dad, I might have to strangle you. I won't ever forgive him for this or for putting my sisters on that fucking plane.

Sadly, however, there's been no news on my family and the Coast Guard is now telling me that they can't do much more. They've searched thousands of square miles between here and the last place the plane made contact near Miami.

"Knock, knock!" It's six a.m. and Elle's head pops through the door of my father's study, where I am going over the paperwork from Larson. Elle's seen everything too, and I'm sure she's come to the same conclusion. Save the big picture or save my family. If they're even still alive.

I can't think of a worse situation.

I paste on a brittle smile. "Good morning, princess."

She steps into the room with a bounce to her step, wearing a light orange dress and white sandals. Her hair is braided into pigtails and she's wearing her usual chunky glasses with tape in the middle.

"Henry?" With a giant grin, she swoops her hands together like she's praying for a miracle. "I have a big proposal for you. And before you say a word, I only want to say that I've been up all night and may or may not have consumed ten Red Bulls, interfering with my motor skills and the ability to control the pace of my speech."

"Errr...okay?" I set down the pen in my hand on the desk. "I'm listening."

"Good! Listening is good! Because what I'm going to say will sound crazy. Like...Fruit Loops on a weekend bender kinda crazy."

"Elle," I interrupt, "please."

"Okay." She holds out her hands. "Okay. Well, I'm sure you've reviewed your father's assets and have come to the same conclusion as I have. He may have been a not so nice person, but he was a rock-solid investor and businessman. I'm actually kind of impressed."

"Please don't praise the man. I'm not ready to go there."

"Oh. Sorry." She takes a rapid breath. "Well, he's been working very hard to diversify into many areas, such as solar, hydro, algae farming, pharma, and even recycling and sustainable lumber. His portfolio is his blueprint for an empire situated to make money as much as solve the world's biggest problems. Which is really cool, but at the same time makes your job of running everything completely impossible. The learning curve is too steep. For you, that is."

"Why do I feel like you're about to insult me?" I grumble.

"Oh, no." She holds out a hand. "I'm not sure I could take it on either. Which is why I talked to the head of legal studies at our university and then I talked to the head of the business department. And then I spoke to the heads of the environment studies, chemistry, agriculture and computer sciences."

"That's a lot of people."

"Right? But I told them all about your situation

and then they called an emergency board meeting at three a.m. and now they're all standing outside this door."

I jerk back my head. "Why?"

"We—I mean—*they* have a proposal for you. According to Professor Boomer, the head of the finance department, there is no way to circumvent the fact that you'll have to raise money to pay taxes when the companies transfer to your name." She holds up a finger. "But...but! Because the companies are not public, you get to choose who you sell the shares to and for how much. That means you can donate up to ten percent of the shares to the university."

I'm not sure I like giving away ten percent of twelve billion dollars, but I'm unsure I have a whole heck of a lot of choices.

Elle holds up a finger. "You gift ten percent to the university instead of selling all of the necessary shares. This way, the deduction helps to wash out some of your tax obligation and they will give you free consulting as part of their owning a stake in everything. Okay, and you allow them to create exclusive internship programs with each of your companies to support the academic programs in various departments. Okay, and you'd have to give me one hundred percent control of everything so that you can go back to school, finish your business degree, and play for the NFL."

"Elle, that dream is dead. I can't—"

"Whoa, cowboy. You can. You just have to decide if you want to be like your dad or let go of control and trust your wife to run it all."

"My wife?"

"Well, I did have a prenup drawn up so that if we don't work out, you keep everything you came into the marriage with, but the tax burden will be slightly less on your inheritance if we marry and file jointly. Plus, legally, it's easier for me to take control of the companies. The only question is whether you want to trust me."

"Of course I do, Elle. That's not a question."

"Then?" she asks.

"There's nothing to share unless my parents are declared dead."

"No, Henry. Not true. That sleazy lawyer lied to you. As the sole inheritor and with the fate of so many jobs and families' well-being on the line, the court can have everything put into a temporary trust and appoint you the executor. You can run things until you feel like all efforts have been exhausted. Then the transfer of ownership can happen later."

Jesus, I love this woman. With a few precise words she's saved my soul from a lifetime of torment.

"Are you sure about all this? I mean, didn't you want to go into physics and math or something?"

"Like I said before, I am a woman of many passions. One is clean energy and you already know your father bought a few companies in that arena.

Desert algae is so sexy! Okay, plus, I'm totally going to start a company so I can build a tele-transporter. And we're going to find a way to make cancer medicines affordable. But this is a chance to do something big, a challenge worthy of my brain power."

"Then yes," I say.

"Yes, what?" she asks.

"Yes, I'll marry you. Today."

She rushes around the desk and throws her arms around my neck. I can't say I've ever been big on hugs, but Elle's touch feels like a ray of warm sunshine on a very dark and stormy night.

"Oh, Henry. Mr. Nucleus is going to be so happy to have a legal daddy!" Her big brown eyes tear up.

Yeah...um...okay. I'm marrying you to make the cat happy. "I thought you wanted to do this because you love me."

"There's that, too." She kisses my lips.

"I love you, too," I say, trying not to laugh.

"Green light, everyone. Henry said yes!" Elle claps her hands and the room fills with people, including Tass and Hunter, who's holding Mr. Nucleus's cat carrier.

"What are you guys doing here?" I ask.

Tassie steps forward wearing a white suit. *Weird.*

"After you hear what these nice people have to say," Tassie says, "we're going to take you and Elle down to the courthouse for your license. Then I'm going to marry you! I got my pastor certificate online yesterday."

And weirder.

"Sounds great." I look at this room filled with a dozen people, including the president of our university. The idea to have them own some of the company is insane. Brilliant and insane. We get access to some of the best academic minds in Texas, who know almost everything about different aspects of these companies, and they get access for their students for some incredible real-life learning. I suspect we're going to be hiring a ton of interns.

My only regret is that my family won't be there to watch us marry. And, even though I know my father wouldn't approve, his absence will be noted because for all his shortcomings, I know deep down inside that he loved us. He just had one hell of a way of showing it, as did my mother.

"You okay, Henry?" Elle asks.

I give my head a shake and glance up at all of these smiling faces. I realize that I am okay, or at least I will be. Because loving Elle is the best decision I've ever made.

"Yeah. I'm symbiotified. All the way."

CHAPTER SIXTEEN
ELLE

Two Months Later.

"Oh, wife. I'm home!" Henry returns from practice, smiling, charged with pheromones, and ready to hump me into the next galaxy.

I set down my pen and push away from the desk in the little corner of his room that now serves as my office. "Looks like someone had a good practice."

"Yes!" He rips off his shirt and immediately starts shimmying down my shorts and panties, nearly tugging me off my chair.

I love how he makes love to me now that the season is officially over. He ended on a high note right before Christmas, signed the contract with his dream team, the Texans, and now just has a few more classes to finish for graduation in May.

"Oh," I say with a saucy voice, pulling off my shirt and bra, "does that mean I get the Henry special?"

He slides off his pants and kicks them into the

corner of his room, in the apartment we now share with Hunter and two other guys despite Henry being the tenth-richest man in the US. He said he wanted to be surrounded by his other family and the location is convenient since it's close to campus, but I think he also just wants to grow up in his own time, on his own terms, and savor every last moment of college. Exactly how life should be. Living each moment to the fullest.

"Don't you worry, little woman. I'm going to give you the Oh-Henry special, with a few extra Os thrown in." He grins with a dimply smile, and I can't help thinking how lucky I am. Life doesn't get much better. My mother's health seems to be improving every day, Henry is back in school and playing football, and I am working with some of the smartest, most determined people I've ever met. So while I might be officially overseeing all of these companies, I'm really just learning how to leverage smart people and raise them up to their fullest potential. We're going to do good things for this world. Really, really good things.

As for Henry's family, the search and rescue teams never found a clue. Not one little piece of wreckage or a body or anything. Henry's entire family simply vanished into thin air and there's not a day that goes by where he doesn't think about them. Some days are better than others, of course, but I try to remind him of the future where it doesn't hurt so much and how everything we're doing would make them proud. Even his disturb-ingly smart dictator of a father. Okay, no, it wouldn't. That man is probably going ballistic in his grave. I mean, he didn't want Henry to marry anyone but Candice. He definitely didn't want Henry going pro. And he would absolutely loathe the idea of a stranger without a college degree running his empire, not to mention giving partial ownership to a university. No. Henry's dad would not approve one little bit. But what else were we supposed to do? Do everything to make his father happy after he's moved on?

Henry scoops me up in his arms like I weigh nothing and then flops me down onto the bed. I love the hungry look in his green eyes and how on the outside he seems so intimidating and strong, but on the inside he's got a playful heart of gold. Of course, he's still able to kick some serious ass and is as stubborn as a mule half the time, but he always makes the right choices in the end.

He lays himself between my thighs and kisses me with a ravenous passion. He's already hard as hell and nudging against my entrance, but I know he'll wait. He's got to warm me up a little to take him.

His hand starts to roam and makes its way to my breast, pinching my already taut nipple. His hips begin rhythmically grinding into my c-spot, igniting that throbbing sensation deep inside. I instantly lose myself in his sweet smell, the softness of his lips and warmth of his naked body covering mine. He was right, we work. Every inch of our bodies and our souls just work like some sort of magical recipe for happiness.

I feel the head of Henry's thick cock nudging a bit deeper, testing my wetness for him.

"I'm almost there," I say, panting my words.

"Oh, God. I just need you so badly."

"Mmmm...I like the sound of you begging." I return to kissing him, placing my hands on his cheeks, savoring the bristles of his short whiskers.

"You want me to beg? You know what you have to do." His voice is gruff and sexy, which makes me amenable to anything he wants.

"Okay, but this is the last time, Henry." I take a breath. "Two plus two is four. Four plus four is eight—"

"Oh, so nerdy." He chuckles. "I can't take it, Elle. Let me fuck you."

"More begging. I want more. Eight plus eight is sixteen—"

His phone rings in some strange high-pitched sound resembling a siren. His entire body freezes.

"What's that?" I ask.

His face sheds all color. "That's the ringtone I set for the police."

I immediately know what this means. They have news. And after two months, there is only one type of news they can possibly give us. They found the bodies.

Henry jumps off me and goes for his pants on the floor, retrieving his phone. "Hello?"

I hold my breath as he turns away. I can see every muscle in his back, ass, and thighs tense up.

Oh no. Oh no. I jump to my feet and pull on my shorts and discarded T-shirt. I then walk around him to see his face. It's an expression I've never quite seen, like he's been kicked in the watermelons.

"You're sure," Henry mutters and then listens some more. "You're fucking sure." Henry slowly walks over to the bed and sits down. "Okay. I'll be right over." He ends the call and stares at the wall.

"What is it? What happened?" I ask.

"They're alive. They're fucking alive," he mutters. "All of them."

TO BE CONTINUED...

Keep turning pages for details about *Digging A Hole*, Book #3 of the Ohellno Series, how to get FREE signed bookmarks, and the Author's Note about this book.

Or GO TO:

www.mimijean.net/diggingahole.html
for buy links, extras, and more!

AUTHOR'S NOTE

Hi Everyone!

Okay, so a teeny, tiny cliffy there, but two things! One, we know that Elle and Henry are now in it together no matter what happens with his father. Two, the "what happens" strongly ties into Book #3, Digging A Hole (Get it? Snort! He's an a-hole, and she's digging him? Or digging his grave? Both? We'll just have to wait and see!) But be sure to sign up for my newsletters so you know what's coming! (Plus, I give away an obscene amount of goodies, so there's always that, too.)

SIGN UP HERE:
for Mimi's mailing list to receive an ALERT for this book!
https://goo.gl/9NZiqR

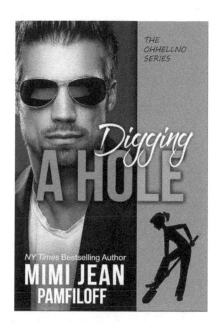

He's the meanest boss ever.
She's the sweet shy intern.
They're about to wreck each other crazy.

My name is Sydney Lucas. I am smart, deathly shy, and one hundred percent determined to make my own way in the world. Which is why I jumped at the chance to intern for Mr. Nick Brooks despite his reputation. After ten failed interviews at other companies, he was the only one offering. Plus, everyone says he knows his stuff, and surely a man as stunningly handsome as him can't be "the devil incarnate," right? Wrong.

Oh...that man. That freakin' man has got to go! I've been on the job one week, and he's insulted my mother, wardrobe shamed me, and managed to make me cry. Twice. Underneath that stone-cold, beautiful face is the evilest human being ever.

But I'm not going to quit. Oh no. For once in my life, I've got to make a stand. Only, every time I open my mouth, I can't quite seem to muster the courage. Perhaps my revenge needs to come in another form: destroying him quietly.

Because I've got a secret. I'm not really just an intern, and Sydney Lucas isn't my real name.

FOR EXTRAS, BUY LINKS, and MORE, GO TO:
www.mimijean.net/diggingahole.html

OKAY! So moving on...

How to get a FREE signed OH, HENRY bookmark.

> **Step #1**: HURRY! (Bookmarks and fridge magnets are on a 1st come basis. When I'm out, I'm out!)
>
> **Step #2**: Email your shipping address to mimi@mimijean.net
>
> **Step #3**: If you LOVED the book and posted a REVIEW, please do mention it! I'll include an extra goodie (generally a magnet) as a thank you.

Next is one of my favorite parts about doing these notes: Explaining what the book is all about! Think you figured it out?

Let's see!

This time there are two underlying themes, inspired by the stuff going on in my real life.

First, my son and I were talking about bullies the other day. Being that he's about to go into middle school, it's not an unusual topic. Now, the schools don't ever want to be seen as advocating fighting. I also don't feel like that's the way to go, considering they're all children. But I also had to recognize and be honest with my son about one important fact: If you don't stand up, bullies just keep coming back for more. Power is like a drug to them. Sadly, I also had to explain that the bullies don't end once you leave school. They're everywhere and come in all ages and genders. So learning to stand your ground, with appropriate force, is part of learning how to deal with people in the real world. Someone hits you in the face, you have a right to defend yourself. If someone is always threatening you, you have the right to do something about it. Simple, right?

Not always. Sometimes there are no easy solutions—a bully boss in a job you need, a bully teacher in a class you have to pass, a family member you love, but who is not always nice. Sometimes there's no easy walking away or a clear path. (And dealing with conflict is not easy for everyone.) But the alternative, doing nothing, will only leave you feeling helpless, and that is not an option either.

Anyway, as you saw, Henry and Elle did not have a clear plan B when it came to dealing with Henry's overbearing dad, but they realized if they didn't stand up, then his father would just keep going, making Henry quit football, making Henry work for him, and pushing a wedding with Candice.

So what next? After Henry believes his father died, Henry tries to put the pain behind him. But now that good old dad is back, they are going to have to face that dragon. Only this time, they'll face him together. There just is no other option, even if they lose, and I think that was the point. We don't always know if we'll win, but if we don't fight, for damn sure we'll lose. Gotta at least try.

The second theme of the book is about love and how sometimes loving someone just isn't enough. I look at the divorce rate in the US and then I look at my parents, who are about to celebrate fifty years of marriage. (Congrats, guys!! Love you!!) I have to wonder what's made them so different? I mean, it's not like all those people who get divorced went into it without love. That's silly. Of course they loved each other. But then, something happens and it falls apart. So for the couples who make it through all the fights, money troubles, power struggles, illnesses, teenaged kids, aging, jealousy, and whatever else life throws at us adults, I have to wonder if it really comes down to commitment and believing that this other person is maybe just a tiny bit better than you. Maybe you have to put your partner on a pedestal? (Not too high, but high enough.)

No, I don't mean it in a self-deprecating way. I mean maybe the trick is seeing that there are these parts of your partner that are incredible and superior to your own traits, which makes you lucky to have them. Because, if you're like me, you tend to think a little too highly of yourself sometimes and wish that everyone could be perfect like you. (So me! Ha-ha.) And then reality sets in, and I see the truth about myself. I'm a rock star at some things, really. But not everything. And it's those little parts of my husband that are so much better than me that remind me that I'm not really "the shit," and he's worth committing to.

Okay, anyway, the point is that maybe you can love someone with all your heart, but it might not be enough. Maybe you really have to be willing to see your imperfections in order to see their perfections. That's really what happened with Elle and Henry, they finally caught a real glimpse of themselves, and then they were able to see each other. Obviously, Elle really had a superwoman superiority complex because of her IQ, and it took looking in the mirror for her to realize she wasn't all that. Then she had to come to terms with the reality of her true strengths, including when and where she could really make a difference. Henry, too, had to face the fact that he couldn't do it all. He needed help.

Anyway, I hope you enjoyed my mental detour and the philosophical bullcrap that goes through my mind when I'm writing these stories!

Until we mind meld again, read long and prosper!

With Love,
Mimi

PLAYLIST

Listen to the soundtrack for this book on SPOTIFY
or grab the songs from here!

PLAYLIST on SPOTIFY:

www.mimijean.net/oh-henry-spotify-music-list.html

"Hey DJ" CNCO
"Filthy/Gorgeous" Scissor Sisters
"We Will Rock You" The Rockers
"Straight Outta Cold Beer" Blake Shelton
"Adventure Of A Lifetime" Coldplay
"Tonight (Best You Ever Had)" John Legend
"La Cucaracha" Los Paisanos
"Sleeping With A Friend" Neon Trees
"Higher (Feat. Maty Noyes)" Lemaitre
"Classic (feat. Powers)" The Knocks
"Wish I Knew You" The Revivalists
"MoneyGrabber" Fitz and the Tantrums
"Getaway" Saint Motel
"Genghis Khan" Miike Snow
"Wish I Knew You" The Revivalists
"Take It or Leave It" Cage The Elephant
"Move" Saint Motel
"Talk Too Much" Coin
"Happy Pills" Weathers

"High And Low" Empire of the Sun

"Ancient Mars" The Zolas

"The Judge" twenty one pilots

"How You Like Me Now (Original)" The Heavy

"Amerika" Young the Giant

"These Days" Dr. Dog

"Nice Try" I Am Arrows

"Cake By The Ocean" DNCE

"Suit And Jacket" Judah & the Lion

"Sweet Talk" Saint Motel

"Benny Goodman" Saint Motel

"You Do It Well" Saint Motel

"Spark" Fitz and the Tantrums

"Brazil" Declan McKenna

"Anna Sun" Walk The Moon

"Cielito Lindo" Ana Gabriel

"Sun" Two Door Cinema Club

"Stand By Your Man" by Tammy Wynette

ACKNOWLEDGEMENTS

A big OH THANK YOU! to the team who continually steps up to tackle my stories: Kylie, Dalitza, Ally, and Naughty Nana. Thank you for the feedback and encouragement all these years!

And, as always, my gratitude goes out to the wonderful professionals who help turn my stories into touchdowns: Latoya, Pauline, Su, and Paul.

AND FINALLY, you guessed it…my dudes! Thank you for the coffee, sandwiches, and chocolate fuel. Book #28! Woohoo!

Thank you!
Mimi

EXCERPT OF SMART TASS

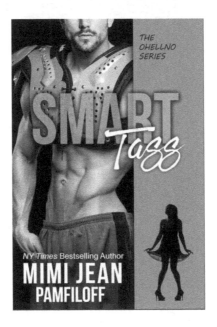

He's the hot college quarterback all the girls want.
She's the smart girl he loves to pick on.
And now that they're all grown up, things are about to get geekin' ugly...

My name is Tass. I'm smart, I'm driven, and I am determined not to let prankster Hunter Johnson continue raining on my parade. When we were little, he'd pull my hair and call me names. When we were teenagers, he'd throw food and tease me for being a flat-chested virgin.

But now that we've ended up at the same college,

he's out of his hot head if he thinks he can keep messing with my life. It's like he's fixated on me or something. Well, guess what, Mr. Amazefootball? I'm not that geeky little girl anymore and you do *not* screw with a smart woman.

So what's my plan?

It's definitely wild, and he's about to find out…

www.mimijean.net/smartass.html

CHAPTER ONE (Smart Tass)

"Jesus, Hunter. You're a bigger piece of shit than I thought," I snap, standing in the middle of the library at Austin U, with the star quarterback kneeling in front of me, his beefy arms wrapped around my legs.

What is he even asking for? Because he hasn't said and I don't know.

"I'm not leaving until you say yes, Tass," he mumbles with his head pressed into my kneecaps. Okay, really his mouth is wedged between my thighs—*not cool!*—so I just pretend we're engaging in kneecap contact.

"Come on, Tassie. It's just one little yes, and I'm gone." His sky-blue eyes gaze up at me with the sincerity of a blow-up doll while the student body chuckles and snaps off pictures.

Wonderful. Let's make a historical record of this mortifying moment.

"Get off me, Hunt! I have to get to class."

He tightens his iron grip, biting down on a shit-eating grin. "Not until you say yeeees," he sings.

I have no clue what he wants, but God, I loathe jocks. I hate the way they laugh at each other's douche-bag jokes. I hate how they strut around like they're God's gift to the universe herself. I hate their obsessions with cheap beer, pickup trucks, and blonde girls in short skirts.

And I especially hate this guy, Hunter Johnson. Aka Hunt. Also referred to by himself and his followers as "The Hunt," "The Man," "Mr. Amaze-football," and my own creation, "Dickhead." Okay. Mine isn't so original, but neither is the dipshit hugging my knees for no other reason than after all these years, he still hopes he'll get a rise out of me. But I wouldn't queef in Hunt's general direction to save his life. Not that I've ever queefed. Or had sex. Or…anything. But, hey, I have my "better than you" scoreboard. Hunt – 1. Tassie – 562.

And just why is my score so high? This game has been going on for as long as I can remember, starting in preschool all the way through high school. Hunter and I were neighbors. Technically, we still are since our parents continue living next door to each other back home.

Lucky me. But imagine my delight when I learned that Hunter and I would be going to the same university.

Both on full scholarships.

Unbelievable. I worked my entire life for straight As. I made sacrifices—mostly to my social life and girlish figure since studying didn't leave room for much else. Hunt, on the other hand, just threw around a ball while wearing tight pants and humping his way through the cheerleading squad.

Fed up with his little game, I reach down and grab a fistful of Hunter's dark brown hair that skirts his annoyingly strong jawline. His hair is longer than he used to wear it back in high school, and it's surprisingly soft, too. *I can make nice earmuffs out of it after I scalp him.*

"Ow! Hey," he squawks, but goes right back to locking up my legs the second I release his silky hair.

"All right," I say through clenched teeth. "What do you want, Hunt?"

"Say yes. That's all. Please, Tass?" His callused fingers press into my bare calves underneath my floral, knee-length skirt. Strangely, his hands feel satisfyingly rough.

What? No. You are not enjoying this.

Hunter's thumbs make tiny circles behind my knees, almost like he's heard my thoughts and agrees with them: *"Yeah, giiiiirl! You know it."*

A silent cringe tears through me.

"Dammit, Hunter," I say, doing a wiggle-step, trying to keep my balance. I'd prefer not to fall over and show the world my Hello Kitty Friday underwear beneath my skirt. "Get off!"

"Would love to." He laughs, wiggling his dark eyebrows. "My place or yours?"

"Har, har, asshole," I say.

"Ouch. Such words, little Tassie." He chuckles

and his breath tickles my inner thighs. It feels oddly intimate, and I don't like it one little bit. "Now, you really have to say yes."

"Yes to *what*? Use your words, tiny man." Tiny refers to his brain, not his body. In the size department, he's a tall, lean, mean football machine. A complete waste of a nice male body.

"I need your help." He makes a pouty face that quickly turns into—

"Nooo. Don't you do it! I'm so not in the mood. Don't you dare use the—"

"Paweeez, Tassie…" His blue eyes are super big and the tip of his pink tongue darts out the side of his mouth.

Oh God. Not the puppy face. I refrain from cracking a smile. He first used it on me when we were five to wheedle a graham cracker. Over the years, he's used it to convince me to do things like lie to his parents—"Yes, Hunt was with me, studying"— or to tutor him with algebra when he was failing. I never understood why I helped him because the guy made my life a living hell. *It's totally the puppy face.* Case in point, it still gives me the uncontrollable urge to laugh. It's just that stupid.

"Hunter, I swear you're the biggest…" Trying not to smile, I notice a few of his football buddies doubled over, cracking their shit up behind a row of books.

My smile vanishes like a wisp of steam over morning coffee—fair trade, French roast—in case you're wondering what I'm imagining dumping over his head at this very moment.

"You bastard," I curse under my breath. "This is some sort of dare, and you're still living in high school. Well, here's a blast from the past!" I manage a small jab-kick just above his knee, which creates enough space for me to land a real kick into his rib and—*ouch! My foot!*—rock-hard abs.

"Tass." He laughs, releasing me and rolling on his side. "Come on…"

There is no justice in this world. Not for women like me who reject this form of juvenile henpecking, just like I reject push-up bras, oppressive dictatorships, and football—okay, basically any sport that pays its athletes millions of dollars while people go hungry. Intelligence is the only currency that matters.

And Hunter Johnson is dumbass broke!

Okay, right about now you're probably asking yourself if I'm one of those nerdy girls who had a crush on the quarterback back in high school and got her heart decimated every time she saw him walking down the hall, because he didn't actually see her.

Oh hell no.

My father is a software engineer who's created six different algorithms to track global-warming patterns, my mother is an award-winning bioengineer working on a cure for cancer—I want to be her someday—and my brother is a tech CEO and millionaire at the ripe old age of twenty-nine. Don't even get me started on my aunts, uncles, and cousins—all doctors or scientists. With my 3.99 GPA and full scholarship to a university that is not Harvard, Yale, or Princeton, I'm the black sheep of the Summerset clan. But for better or worse, that's my family, and I love them. Even if their standards are incredibly high. Either way, there is zero, and I mean *zero* interest in sports or men of sports on my part.

Hunter especially.

So exactly what *is* the rub between me and him? I'll have to get to that later, because right now, I need to flee from this giant, six-foot-two turd who's determined to latch onto my crotch zone and embarrassed the hell out of me.

I push my glasses back up my nose and head quickly for the exit, praying that no one in my chemistry club has witnessed the altercation, but knowing the library is their turf and the chances of this moment not coming up at tomorrow's study group are nil.

"Great. Just great," I mumble to myself and throw my weight into the heavy steel door to go outside.

"I just want to fuck you, Tass! I need a virgin!" Hunt yells out.

A gust of hot sticky September air flows over me as I pause mid-step in the doorway, wondering if I've actually heard his words correctly.

No, the boy who beat the hell out of Kurt Lipmann in the eleventh grade, defending my honor, would not sink so low. But I'm not stupid, hard of hearing, or delusional. *Yep.* This cave-dwelling crustacean actually said what I think, and from the roaring laughter radiating inside the library, I know everyone else heard him, too.

Wow. Now I'm pissed.

I slowly turn to face my nemesis, who's standing with a gloating grin baked onto his piehole. He thinks he's got me. He thinks I'm going to lose it right here in front of all these people.

Not today, Huntie baby. My self-worth doesn't come from his approval or my sexual status. *I am a strong, smart woman.*

I take a deep breath, let it out, and return with a lifted chin and confident strides. "But Hunter, did your concussion-warped mind forget? You already fucked me. You did it to me in kindergarten and every year of my life since."

Ewwws! and *yucks* erupt from the theater of onlookers. Yeah, I know I made it sound like he had sex with me when I was six. *Nasty!* And point for me. *Tassie – 566.*

I go on, using a sweet, calm voice to twist the knife, "So now that we've established you've achieved your perverted goal, I think you should consider fucking yourself next. In that giant asshole of yours. Oh, but wait. Your shrimp dick won't reach." I make a pouty face and hold up my pinky.

"Poor Hunter. But at least I'm technically still a virgin because of it, which allows me to be deflowered by a real man someday."

His cocky grin morphs into a flat pair of lips and twitching blue eyes.

He's pissed. Another point me.

I sigh contentedly, turn, and exit the library.

Brains beat brawn every time.

FOR INFO, EXTRAS, BUY LINKS and MORE, GO TO:

www.mimijean.net/smartass.html

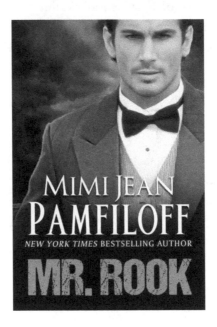

He's Enigmatic, Dangerously Handsome, and COMPLETELY OFF-LIMITS...

The women who vacation on Mr. Rook's exclusive island are looking for one thing and one thing only: to have their wildest romantic fantasies come to life. Pirates, cowboys, billionaires—there's nothing Rook's staff can't deliver.

But when Stephanie Fitzgerald's sister doesn't return after her week in paradise, Stephanie will have to pose as a guest in order to dig for answers. Unfortunately, this means she'll need to get close to the one thing on the island that's not on the menu: the devastatingly handsome and intimidating Mr. Rook. And he's not about to give the island's secrets away.

PROLOGUE (Mr. Rook)

My name is Stephanie Fitzgerald. I am twenty-six years old, London born, New York raised, and I know exactly three things about my current situation.

One: I am an imposter riding on this private jet carrying myself and eleven other women to an island "paradise."

Two: I have no clue what I will find when I disembark, because this exclusive resort doesn't exactly advertise.

Three: I will be fired if I don't return home with concrete information regarding Mr. Rook, the mysterious owner of the island. And when I say I'll be fired, I really mean that my body will be thrown down a deep dark well by a bad, bad man.

Those three things, however, don't really matter. Only finding my sister does. Because the last place Cici was seen alive is here, "Fantasy Island." Yep, that's what some people actually call it. Some even say the show in the '80s was based on this place.

Sure. If your fantasy is to disappear, leaving your family an emotional train wreck, then okay, I concede the point.

Regardless, this is where Cici went after winning a mystery dream vacation in the back of some travel magazine, and it's touted as the real deal. You pay fifty K. They make your wildest fantasies come true. One week in Heaven.

Heaven, my ass.

As the tires hit the wet landing strip and the plane slows to a crawl, I glance out the tiny oval window to my left, and my breath hitches. Standing among the lush vegetation lining the runway is a tall man with square shoulders. He's looking right at me, and those eyes—so predatory, so cold—are the only thing I can really see of him.

I blink, and he vanishes like a wisp of steam.

Fuck. What was that? A hard shiver slams through me as I realize I have no clue what I've just gotten myself into. Because I am one of the next happy guests at Mr. Rook's private island, where "Every woman's fantasy is our business." *And not everyone comes home from vacation.*

CHAPTER ONE (Mr. Rook)

Like its mysterious owner, Rook's Island was practically an urban legend. No brochures. No real website. They advertised strictly by *whisper* of mouth. In other words, you had to know someone willing to tell you about it. Confidentially.

But from the bits and pieces I'd gathered off the Internet, I deduced it was an uncharted island somewhere west of the Bermuda Triangle in Bahaman waters, likely northwest of Highborne Cay among a cluster of unnamed isles. That said, no one could tell you exactly where it was, and if they knew, they'd never admit it. Even the employees of the Bahaman government had simply stared at me like I was a madwoman.

"There is nothing in those waters, ma'am, except fish," one of the clerks from the Bahaman embassy in DC had said several months ago.

"Then why the hell did my sister have a *goddamned* plane ticket to the island?"

The man had simply shrugged. "I cannot say, ma'am. I have never heard of such a place, so perhaps your sister simply lied. People disappear on purpose all the time."

What the fuck? Cici, my sister, was a goddamned saint, a kindergarten teacher who loved her life. She lived for those kids and was the kind of person who made everyone smile.

Unlike me. I used to be outgoing and optimistic, but now I'm just broken. I'm broken because I loved my big sister more than anything. She was my best friend, my blood, and my hero. She was there for me when my widowed father was too busy working and I was trying to grow up without a mother. Cici made us a family, and now she was gone. Just like that. A fact the police had little to say about since they had a video of her clearing out her safe deposit box.

"She did not abandon us, you piece of shit!" I had screamed at the embassy guy. "Now help me fucking find her!"

The rest of that moment—a blur, really— consisted of multiple expletives, resulting in my being arrested and banned from their embassy. Indefinitely. My father, an award-winning war correspondent, had to pull a few strings to get me out of jail that day.

"Stephanie, please don't do this to me," he'd said, his thinning gray hair its usual mess, his strong hands wrapped tightly around the steering wheel of his Volvo—an old beige thing he'd purchased for my mother right before she died. God rest her beautiful soul. She had been a journalist like my dad when they met in Afghanistan, but they moved around a lot for work, eventually landing in New York right after I came along. Then one morning, she was out for a jog and dropped dead of a heart attack. Poof. Gone forever from our lives.

My poor father was never right in the head again, and until this day, he refused to let go of my mom or that Volvo. So while I never really knew her, I felt the painful void she'd left behind, which was why I couldn't give up searching for Cici or accept that there was no island.

And look. There it is... I glanced out the tiny window of the plane, knowing I was one step closer to getting answers.

My heart hammered against my rib cage as the private jet's outer door popped open. Okay, really, my heart hadn't stopped hammering since I'd boarded. What kind of place doesn't require a visa or passport? *A shady place, that's what.*

"Ladies," said the stewardess with dark brown hair matching my own, "the staff here at Mr. Rook's island would like to welcome you to your dream vacation. As you exit the plane, please be careful descending the staircase. Of course," she giggled, "if you do decide to fall, there will be a strong, hand-some gentleman waiting to catch you."

The female passengers, who'd been sipping fancy cocktails since we boarded at a private airfield south of Newark, started clapping and hooting.

"I'm definitely taking a dive, then!" barked out a redhead in her mid-forties, wearing an animal print blouse, white jeggings, and a heavy amount of gold jewelry around her neck. Her accent screamed Southerner, while her outfit screamed new money and that she liked borrowing clothes from her daughter—the one she'd been talking about nonstop to the other passenger directly behind me. Apparently, the redhead had just got divorced from her wealthy cheating husband and the daughter recently graduated from college. This vacation was her big indulgence after years of marital ugliness. The woman to her side, a timid little blonde thing, didn't say much other than her sister had come to Rook's Island over a decade ago and hadn't stop talking about it since.

"I can't wait to meet Mr. Rook," said the redhead. "I hear he's the most delicious thing on the island."

"My sister only saw him once because he didn't mingle much with the guests," said the blonde lady.

"Well," said the redhead with a sassy voice, "if he's as good looking as my friends say, I'm changing my fantasy to a night with him."

In the back of my mind, I tried to understand how these women could actually pay money to come all the way here and sleep with strange men in a weeklong, role-playing, fantasy vacation. It felt so strange to me.

"What's your fantasy this week, sweetheart?" the

redhead asked, staring at me with her mascara-caked eyes.

"Who, me?" I pointed to my chest.

"Yeah. You gonna do some pirate fantasy? Oh wait. I know. You look like the superhero kind." She snapped her fingers. "Thor. You went for the Thor fantasy, didn't ya? I heard he has the biggest *hammer* in the world." She winked.

Nice. Real nice. And why had she made that assessment about me? My look didn't scream cosplay-lover. It didn't scream anything, really. Most men— my exes—would describe me as having classic beauty. I would describe myself as average. Average-length brown hair with average waves. Average brown eyes. Average five foot four height. Average ten pounds overweight. Average intelligence.

My special feature was my tenacity. Once I set out to do something, I achieved my goal no matter how difficult. For example, when I was eight and Cici was fourteen, I decided that our yard needed a treehouse. My father said he was too busy, so I put up a lemonade stand every weekend for five months until I raised enough money to hire a handyman. I got my damned treehouse.

I smiled politely at the redhead and mousy blonde who waited for my reply. "I, uh, really just want flowers, a candlelit dinner on a yacht, and cuddling by the fire—your basic romance," I lied.

They looked at me like I was out of my soft skull for choosing something so tame. But I wasn't here for wild. I was here to find Cici.

"Well, that's cute," said the redhead.

"I'm doing Tarzan," said the blonde, staring at the floor.

I tried to keep a straight face. I couldn't picture this shy little thing swinging through the trees in a suede bikini.

"Sounds…" I swallowed, "dangerous."

"I knooow." Her brown eyes lit with joy.

The line began to clear out of the cabin, so I grabbed my backpack and purse and faced forward.

"Well, enjoy your romantic candles…?" Redhead wanted to know my name.

I glanced over my shoulder. "Stephanie."

"Nice to meet you. I'm Meg," she said and then jerked her head toward the blonde, "and she's Emily."

"Nice meeting you, too," I replied politely.

"We'll see you at the welcome dinner tonight!" Meg said. "I hear the dancers are amazing—ripped from head to toe and almost naked in those Hawaiian grass skirt things."

"Mmmm. Can't wait." I didn't give a crap about dancers or dinners. I wanted to find this Mr. Rook and start asking about Cici. I was ready to put a goddamned knife to his throat if that was what it took.

"Right this way, ladies!" said the overly peppy air stewardess.

One by one, we filed down the rollaway staircase. I immediately noticed the tropical summer heat, the never-ending stretch of lush green jungle, and the musty smell of moist dirt mixed with salty air.

My mind immediately jumped to my sister— her bright smile and big brown eyes. She had been right here on this island, on this very fucking staircase. *What did they do to her?*

My heart bubbled with rage. *Stay in character, Steph. You're a happy guest, like everyone else.* The last thing I wanted was to go ballistic and get kicked off the island before I got what I needed—the truth for myself and information for "my boss," Warner Price. I used the term loosely because Warner and I had more of an arrangement rather than an employer-employee situation. Either way, I couldn't and wouldn't go home until I had what I needed.

Wearing black leather sandals and a long blue cotton dress, I carefully descended the narrow staircase, feeling my anxiety well inside my shaky knees.

"Welcome, Miss...?" Holding out his hand, next to the bottom step, stood a huge tree trunk of a man wearing a blue-and-white Hawaiian shirt and khaki shorts. He had to be at least seven feet tall, his brown skin covered in Samoan tattoos. Even his neck and the back of his shaved head were inked.

"Ms. Brenna," I lied, and shook his large hand. "Let me guess. You must be Tattoo and you tell everyone when the plane arrives?" *This place is a fucking joke.*

He smiled and flashed a set of bright white teeth. "My name is Gerry, ma'am, and our control tower texts the employees to alert us when the guests arrive. May I help you with your things?"

"No." I smiled politely, smoothing down the front of my wrinkled dress, trying my best not to show him the hate inside me. Because for all I knew, he'd had something to do with Cici's death.

No. Don't think that. She's not dead. Sadly, however, my heart knew she would not leave us. Not like that. Which naturally led to one conclusion: She never made it off this island alive.

I held back a snarl and substituted it with a grin. "I can carry my own things, but thanks."

"Very good, Ms. Brenna." Tattoo—I mean Gerry—dipped his shaved head. "Please follow the red carpet to the gravel path. The signs will direct you to the reception building, where our staff will check you in."

"Thanks."

Gerry turned his attention to the next guest behind me—Meg—and I continued on the red carpet, squinting from the hot summer sun beating down on the top of my head.

My first impression of the place was that everything felt too perfect, like a movie set or theme park. Yes, the tall trees were real, and the birds of paradise sprouting from beds of bright red and yellow flowers were real, too, but even the gravel path I followed through the dense jungle didn't have a single pebble out of place.

As I walked, the muted giggles and laughter of the ladies behind me echoed through the trees. All I felt was my skin crawling and those eyes—from the shadow—still watching me.

Stop it, I told myself. *You're letting your imagination get to you.*

I slid my cell from my purse to check for texts or messages from my dad. *Crap. No bars? Not even one little flicker?* I guess I wasn't surprised. This island couldn't stay a secret if people were posting their location on Facebook along with vacation pics.

After a very short walk, the shaded path ended at a large, two-story house with an enormous porch and hanging flowers of every color imaginable. It reminded me of those old coffee plantation homes with whitewash paint and pillars.

I walked up the steps to the porch, my body already dripping with sweat. "Jesus, this place is like living inside a wet volcano," I muttered. I couldn't say I was a fan of humidity before this and now I absolutely loathed it.

I stepped inside the house, where a gentle breeze from the ceiling fans drifted against my hot skin, giving some relief. The white wood-paneled room had fresh flowers atop two white desks, where two pleasant-looking women awaited us. *Oh, look. We're being checked in to heaven.* Every perfect detail of this shitty place pissed me off.

The guests formed a line and then gave their names to the women in blue-and-white blouses behind the desks. After that, another woman, different every time, quickly whisked them off down a hallway.

My turn. I stepped up, feeling nervous as hell. I wasn't great at lying, but there was no other way. *I'm a guest. A happy guest.*

"Hi. I'm Stephanie Brenna."

The young woman with cocoa skin and her black hair pulled into a neat ponytail smiled and then checked my name off her list. "There you are, Ms. Brenna. Julie will be checking you in and going over the island's amenities and rules during your stay."

Julie, a brunette wearing white shorts and the standard Hawaiian blouse, appeared with a bright smile. "Ms. Brenna, hello. Please come right this way."

"What is this?" The whole whisking people away and separating the guests made me uneasy.

The receptionist continued smiling like she was high on life or had just gotten her wings. "Ah, yes. Well, our check-in process is a little different than your standard resort." She leaned into her desk and whispered, "Because of the *unique* nature of our services." She winked.

"So you mean there's sex paperwork," I said.

She pointed her pencil at me. "You got it. And a safety orientation."

"And Mr. Rook? When do I get to meet him?" I asked.

The smiles on the women's faces melted so fast, one might have assumed I'd just told them I'd like to eat their livers.

"What?" I asked. "This is his island, isn't it?"

Julie, my check-in hostess, swallowed something in her throat. "I'm afraid that Mr. Rook doesn't manage the day-to-day operations of the island— he's a very busy man. However, if you have any concerns or needs—anything at all—I will be your personal concierge for the week." Her fake smile reappeared. "And if there's anything I can't manage, the island's executive manager, Mrs. Day, can see to it."

"So I won't get to meet the famous Mr. Rook?" I asked.

They smiled politely, but didn't speak. I got the distinct impression that they were not allowed to say no to a guest.

"All right. Is he even on the island?" I prodded.

The receptionist offered me a bone. "Mr. Rook does have a personal residence here, but we are not kept informed of his schedule or whereabouts. Is there anything we can address? Any concerns?"

The two women eyed the line of rowdy drunk guests behind me. Apparently, one of them had to pee, a fact she happily shared with us all.

Okay, well, if Mr. Rook didn't run things on a daily basis, then he wasn't the only person with answers. Of course, the big boss would have to know if a guest went missing, so I would still need to meet him.

"No." I flashed a smile to make nice. "No concerns at this time."

"Then follow me!" Julie turned for the hallway. "In a few short minutes, I'll have you on your way to a week of pure pampering and relaxation."

"Fabulous." I followed behind her.

"Unless your version of relaxation requires something more vigorous." She glanced over her shoulder and winked.

What's with the damned winking? This entire place gave me the heebie-jeebies. "Can't wait."

FOR INFO, EXTRAS, BUY LINKS and MORE GO TO:
www.mimijean.net/rook.html

ABOUT THE AUTHOR

San Francisco native MIMI JEAN PAMFILOFF is a *USA Today* and *New York Times* bestselling romance author. Although she obtained her MBA and worked for more than fifteen years in the corporate world, she believes that it's never too late to come out of the romance closet and follow your dream. Mimi lives with her Latin lover hubby, two pirates-in-training (their boys), and the rat terrier duo, Snowflake and Mini Me, in Arizona. She hopes to make you laugh when you need it most and continues to pray daily that leather pants will make a big comeback for men.

Sign up for Mimi's mailing list for giveaways and new release news!

STALK MIMI:
www.mimijean.net
twitter.com/MimiJeanRomance
pinterest.com/mimijeanromance
instagram.com/mimijeanpamfiloff
facebook.com/MimiJeanPamfiloff